A King Production presents...

Men Of The Bitch Series...

A Novel

JOY DEJA KING

This novel is a work of fiction. Any references to real people, events, establishments, or locales are intended only to give the fiction a sense of reality and authenticity. Other names, characters, and incidents occurring in the work are either the product of the author's imagination or are used fictitiously, as those fictionalized events and incidents that involve real persons. Any character that happens to share the name of a person who is an acquaintance of the author, past or present, is purely coincidental and is in no way intended to be an actual account involving that person.

ISBN 10: 1942217080
ISBN 13: 978-1942217084
Cover concept by Joy Deja King

Library of Congress Cataloging-in-Publication Data;
A King Production
Nico Carter: Men Of The Bitch Series by Joy Deja King
For complete Library of Congress Copyright info visit:
www.joydejaking.com
Twitter: @joydejaking

A King Production
P.O. Box 912, Collierville, TN 38027

A King Production and the above portrayal logo are trademarks of
A King Production LLC

This Book is Dedicated To My:

Family, Readers and Supporters.
I LOVE you guys so much. Please believe that!!

—Joy Deja King

"I've been in this game for years, it made me an animal, there's rules to this shit so I wrote me a manual..."

—Notorious BIG

A KING PRODUCTION
Nico Carter
Men Of The Bitch Series
JOY DEJA KING

Chapter 1

I Got A Story To Tell

I came into this world wanting one thing... love. I couldn't get that love from my mother so I stole it from the streets. Eventually, I did get the love, respect, and money I craved, but it came at a very high price. As I stand here today, I can't help but ask myself, was it worth it? But before I can answer that question and move forward, I have to go back to what brought me here.

"Nico, get yo' ass in this house," my mother yelled out the window.

"I'm coming!" I yelled back for the third time, running with the ball in my hands, knowing I was lying again. We were playing the hood version of football and my team was winning so I didn't want to stop. See, the older boys in the neighborhood thought they could kick our ass 'cause we were young.

My boy Lance and I were only 10, but we were both tall for our age, fast, and already had a lil' muscle tone. My best friend, Ritchie, and the other boys on our team were either below average or average at best. But with Lance and my skills and the other boys just following our lead, we would constantly beat the older boys. It would drive them crazy and I loved it.

"Touch down!" I hollered and started doing my signature two-step dance move before throwing the ball down. "Peace out motherfuckers!" I grinned, before running towards my apartment.

"We see you tomorrow!" I heard Ritchie and the other boys yell back.

"Boy, you see what time it is?" my mother popped as soon as I closed the door. "You know you ain't supposed to be outside when it get this dark."

"Sorry. I was playing football and didn't realize it was so late."

"Well go in there and get yo'self cleaned up. Yo' daddy will be over here in a little bit," my mom said, fixing her hair in the mirror.

"Now it makes sense," I mumbled.

"What you say, boy?" my mother said, shooting me one of her evil looks.

"I just said I was hungry," I lied.

"I'm sure yo' daddy will take us out to eat when he gets here. So hurry up! I want you to be clean, dressed, and ready when he walk through that door."

I was wondering why my mom was so concerned about me coming in the house. Normally, I could come home at any time of the night and she wouldn't notice or care. She would assume I was at Ritchie's house or another kid in the building and it almost felt like she preferred I stayed there. The only time she wanted me around was if my father was coming over to visit. She would always put on this big show as if she was the Mother Of The Year. I would play along because part of me was always hoping that maybe one day her pretending would rub off and become a reality.

After taking a bath, I decided to put on the New York Knicks jersey my dad had gotten me. I smiled looking at myself in the mirror. I was the spitting image of my father and that made me feel proud.

"Where my lil' man Nico at!" I heard my father call out.

"What up, Dad!" I said, running up to him. He wrapped his strong arms around me giving me a hug like only he could.

"I just saw you a couple days ago and you already grew a few inches. Damn, you a handsome kid, if I say so myself." My dad smiled proudly.

"You only saying that 'cause he look just like you." My mother laughed.

"But of course. Nico know where he get them good looks from, don't you boy," my dad teased, putting his huge hand on top of my head and playfully shaking it. "You ready to go?"

"Yes, sir. Where we going?"

"I got us tickets to go see the Yankees play."

"No way!"

"Do I ever lie to you?"

"Nope, you sure don't, Daddy."

"And I never will. Now let's get outta here."

"Nico said he was hungry. I thought the three of us would go get something to eat," my mother said, folding her arms.

"Maybe next time, Shaniece. Tonight it's just me and my son," my dad said, taking my hand. When I turned to tell my mother bye, she was rolling her eyes.

"What you mean maybe next time? Don't you see me dressed? You think I got all jazzed up to sit in this apartment?"

"Here, go out and have a good time wit' your girlfriends. Nico can stay with me for the night," my dad said, giving my mother a bunch of money. She balled it up in her fist tightly, but I could tell she was steaming mad.

"Fine, you keep him, but you still owe me dinner," she snapped, putting her other hand on her hip.

"See you tomorrow, Mom," I said about to go give her a hug goodbye, but she walked away. I took my dad's hand and we left.

My dad had recently bought a new gold, two door Mercedes Benz sedan and this was the first time I was going for a ride in it. Last week when he stopped by so I could see it, everybody went crazy on the block. My dad was the man and when I grew up I wanted to be just like him. After we got in the car and settled in my dad turned on the radio. But before I could start jamming to the beat, he turned the music down and looked at me.

"Nico, I want you to know something," he said with a stone face. My dad was always smiling and joking so it was weird seeing him so serious.

"What is it, Dad?"

"You're my son, my only child and I love you no matter what."

"I know and I love you, too."

"You might not be seeing me around at your mother's place that much anymore, but I want you to come stay at my house on the weekends. Is that okay with you?"

"Yes! I just wanna spend time with you. I don't care where."

"That's my boy. Now let's go see these Yankees." My dad smiled and drove off.

Although I was young, I knew exactly what was going on. Ever since I could remember my mother and father were on and off. They never lived together and half the time they were arguing and the other half they were in the bedroom with the door locked. I guess they were about to be off again. My dad had never told me he wasn't going to be coming around, so something had changed, I just didn't know what.

Chapter 2

Family Ties

"Motherfucker, you think 'cause you got a new bitch that shit done change! Please, yo' ass will be back like always! But in the meantime don't think you gon' be gettin' my son on the weekends!" I heard my mom scream to my dad. I closed my bedroom door not wanting to hear the arguing, but my mom was being extra loud tonight so I had no choice, but to hear every word. My dad, who was normally so chill, was even amped up.

"Shaniece, that's our son and yes the fuck I will be getting him every weekend. Try to keep Nico away from me and see how real shit get for you."

"Is that a threat, motherfucker? Is you threatening me? Let me pick up the gotdamn phone right now and call the fuckin' police so I can let them know my baby daddy is threatening me."

"Put that phone down!" I heard my father holler. Then I heard what sounded like a small tussle. "Give me the phone, Shaniece!"

"I ain't giving you shit!" I heard what sounded like some more scuffling, so I ran out my room to see what was going on. When I got in the living room I saw my mother slam the telephone on the side of my father's head.

"Fuuuuuuck!" my dad yelled out in pain as he held his head. "You lucky I don't put my hands on no woman," he said, wiping away some blood that was dripping down the side of his face.

"Go 'head hit me! You supposed to be so big and bad. Give it yo' best shot," my mother cracked trying to provoke my father into a fight. As if feeling my presence my mother turned in my direction. "Nico, go back in yo' room!"

"Daddy, are you okay?" I asked, concerned about my father.

"I'm fine, son."

"Don't worry 'bout yo' daddy. He a grown man. Now get yo' ass back in yo' room."

I heard what my mother said, but I couldn't move. I felt like my dad needed me. I didn't know what I could do to help, but I thought standing here, where he could see me, somehow let him know that I was on his side.

"I ain't gon' tell you again, Nico. Go to your

room!" my mother screamed like she had lost her mind.

"Go 'head son. Go to your room. I'm fine. I'll come check on you before I leave," my father said, trying to console me. I put my head down and went back to my room. I didn't close my door though because I had now become fixated on wanting to hear every single word.

"Royce, don't make this get ugly. You go 'head and have fun wit' yo' new bitch and when you ready to get yo' shit together, you can come back to your family. But Nico will not be spending the weekends at your house. If you want to see him, you can come over here."

"If you want to keep a roof over your head, food on the table, a car parked outside, and clothes on your back you will let me have my son on the weekends. Do you understand me?" my father warned.

"You saying you would cut me off? If I don't eat then yo' son don't eat."

"My son is going to eat just fine. He ain't gon' neva starve, but you won't have nothing. If you do have something, it won't be coming from me. The choice is yours, but either way, I will have my son. I don't have to lay a finger on you to let you know that I mean every single word."

"Fuck you, Royce! You gon' pay for this shit!!" my mother yelled, but instead of responding to her, he came to my bedroom.

"I'm sorry you had to hear all that, son," my

father said, giving me a hug.

"It's not your fault."

"It's not your mother's fault either. She just can't help herself," my dad said jokingly and then laughed, trying to put a smile on my face. "I'll be here on Friday to pick you up so be ready."

"I will! You promise?" My eyes lit up, excited by the idea of spending the entire weekend at my dad's house for the first time.

"Yes, I promise. See you soon. Love you, lil' man."

"I love you too, Daddy." I hugged my dad one more time, extra tight and watched him walk out the door.

Like my father always did, he kept his promise. He came to get me that weekend and every weekend after that. When he arrived my mom would be standing at the front door with a frown on her face, her arms folded and hand out. It was as if she was selling me off to my dad every weekend. It was then that I realized all women had a price, including mothers.

"Nico, do you want me to make you some more spaghetti?" Chrissy, my dad's girlfriend, asked.

"No, thanks, I'm good."

"Okay, but if you need anything let me know.

I'll be in the kitchen."

"I will. Thanks." I smiled when Chrissy walked away. Although she was a lot older than me, that woman was fine. She had the smoothest chocolate-colored skin I had ever seen which made her per-fectly-white, straight teeth sparkle even more. Not only was she fine, but she was nice. She treated my father like a king and me like a little prince. I now understood why my dad had moved on from my mom and kept Chrissy around permanently... she was what I would hear old heads call, a keeper.

As the years passed, I began to think of Chris-sy as a mother figure. Honestly, she seemed to love me more than my own mother. She gave me that affection I never got from my mother and it seemed genuine. I wanted to move in with them full time, but my mother wasn't having it. I don't think it was so much that my mother wanted me around, but because she didn't want the cash to stop coming in from my father. I had become a steady paycheck for her and she had no intentions of letting that go.

"How you like Chrissy?" my dad asked out the blue while we were riding in his car, on our way to Marvin's house, who was like a brother to my dad and I called uncle. I loved when my dad would let me hang out with him when he had running around to do. I would listen to all the small talk him and his friends would make and learned so much about the streets. I was fascinated and wanted to be them, al-though my father was adamant I would go to college.

"You know I like Chrissy. She makes the best sweet potato pie, too." I grinned, nodding my head, thinking about how good that last slice I had tasted.

"Boy, I know she can cook, but do you like her? I mean, really like her?"

"I more than like her, I love her, Dad." I noticed my dad's eyes get a little glassy. "Dad, are you okay?"

"I'm better than okay. I'm just so happy you said that, because I didn't want to ask her to be my wife unless you approved. We partners you know." He smiled before shaking my hand.

"You're finally going to get married?"

"If Chrissy accepts my proposal."

"You know she will. Chrissy has wanted to be your wife for a long time."

"How you know that?"

"That day she had to pick me up from school early because I had gotten sick and I couldn't get in touch with Mom. Well, when I was leaving one of the kids asked me was that my mother and I said no, she's my dad's wife. I thought you all were already married."

"You did?"

"Yep. I mean you been living together for the last few years. But when I said that, Chrissy smiled and told me she wasn't your wife yet, but hopefully one day soon. That's how I know she'll accept your proposal."

"Good, because after we stop by Marvin's place

we're going to go pick up the ring. I'm popping the question tonight."

"Does that mean I can live with you all the time now?" I wanted to know.

"I would love that, son, but convincing your mother is another story."

"If anybody can convince her, it's you."

"I'll work on it."

"You promise?" I knew if I made my dad promise that meant he would do his best because my father never liked to make a promise and not keep it.

"I promise," he said and winked his eye. After my dad said that I sat back in my seat and relaxed for the rest of the car ride. He was like a superhero to me and now that he made a promise I knew he would make my wish come true.

"Shaniece, listen, I wanted to talk to you about something," my dad said when he brought me home after one of my weekend visitations. Instead of going to my bedroom, I sat down on the living room couch and started rumbling through my overnight bag like I was looking for something. I was hoping he was finally going to ask her about me living with him full time, since it had been weeks since I asked him to.

"What is it?" my mom replied with her arms

folded tightly, giving off major attitude. I already knew this wasn't going to go well, but I didn't care because I wanted out.

"I was thinking that maybe it would be best if Nico come live with me. I mean, he just turned 13 so he's a teenager now. I think I'll be a good influence for him."

"A good influence... what you gon' teach him? How to sell drugs?" she smacked. "You gon' teach my son how to make money by being a street hustler like you?"

"You don't seem to have a problem taking my money. Since it's good enough for you, I think we need to leave the subject of me selling drugs alone. Nico will be well taken care of in my home."

"Who gon' take care of him? That little bitch you got engaged to? Yeah, I heard you asked that heffa to marry you. So the woman that pushed out your first-born son wasn't good enough for you to put a ring on, but you married some gold-digging hussy. If you think you gon' take my son and my money, you must be motherfuckin' crazy."

"First off, leave my fiancé out of this. Secondly, our son is not a paycheck. But because he will be coming to see you I don't have a problem still giving you money. It may not be as much, but we can work out something."

"We ain't working out shit! Nico ain't going nowhere. I'll see yo' ass in court first. Ain't no judge gonna take a son away from their mother, and give custody to a drug dealer. So you and yo' fiancé go have yo' own baby, 'cause this one right here," my mother turned and pointed to me, "ain't going nowhere."

"Well, I guess I'll be seeing you in court, Shaniece. But I advise you to get your own house in order, 'cause I ain't the only one with skeletons. I'll see you Friday, Nico."

"Okay, Dad... love you."

"Love you, too," he said before closing the door behind him.

I could feel my mother staring at me, but I refused to look up. I kept going through my bag until she walked away. I had never seen her so angry, but inside I was smiling. I got absolutely no happiness living with her. I loved my mother because I thought it was the right thing to do. I believed that you were supposed to love the woman that brought you into this world even if there wasn't a nurturing bone in her body. I wanted to live with my father and I was positive that one way or another my dad would make that my reality.

Chapter 3

The Moment I Feared

"I'm so sick of this shit," I said to Ritchie as we were walking home from school.

"You always complaining. What you sick about now?"

"Living with my mom, going to school, doing homework. That same shit over and over again."

"Man, you don't even do no homework. You be letting Kecia or one of your other lil' girlfriends do it for you."

"'Cause that homework shit is a waste of time. When we go out in these streets and make money ain't nobody gon' be asking us about science, history, and that other crap. All we need to know is math so we can count our fuckin' money."

"Whatever, Nico. Yo' pops already said you wouldn't be hustling in them streets. We supposed to go to college, remember."

"Fuck that. College ain't for me. I'm in 8th grade and already tryna come up with a way to get out of it, so you know college is out the question."

"Yo' pops will kick yo' ass. And you know yo' moms ain't having it."

"Like my mom would care. As long as I don't bother her and interrupt her flow she don't give a fuck what I do. I'm just a way of her getting money from my dad."

"That ain't true," Ritchie said half-heartedly.

"All my mom do is run the streets with yo' mom. My mom only pretend like she give a fuck when my pops come around so she can keep getting money from him."

Ritchie tried to pretend not hear what I said because he was in denial. He knew his mom was the same way, but he only wanted to see the best in her. That was a major difference between the two of us. I looked at the world for what it was, the good, bad, and ugly. Ritchie, on the other hand, wanted to remain a kid forever and view the world from the eyes of a child.

"So are we hooping this weekend or what," Ritchie said, changing the subject. Sometimes on the weekends Ritchie would come stay at my dad's with me, but I wasn't sure if I wanted him to come this time.

"I might, but nah if I can get in on this dice game that kid Manny have going on."

"Dice? You mean like gambling?"

"Yes, you square ass nigga, gambling. I need to get my money up. If only my pops would let me work one of his corners I wouldn't have to play no dice."

"You bet not let yo' dad find out you playing dice," Ritchie said, shaking his head.

"And you bet not open yo' big ass mouth and say nothing," I warned, tossing a rock at his back.

"Ouch, that hurt." Ritchie sighed.

"Stop whining before I throw another one and hit you in the head." I laughed.

"You betta not!"

"I betta not what?" I yelled, as I started chasing him home. We both laughed as Ritchie almost tripped and fell, but we kept running. Right when I got up on Ritchie to throw him to the ground, we stopped in our tracks noticing a bunch of cops surrounding our apartment complex.

"What's going on?" I asked a crack head who was standing off to the side, watching everything.

"Somebody got killed. That's all I know. The cops questioning everybody," he said, seeming antsy.

"Come on, let's find out what's going on," Ritchie said, grabbing my arm. I picked up my backpack and followed him over to the large crowd that was gathered in a circle.

"Yo, that kid just rolled up and shot him and

rolled out," I heard a local neighborhood man say.

"I know, the shit happened so fast, I don't even remember what he looked like," another dude said.

"Look, that must be the body over there," Ritchie said, nudging my arm. He pointed towards the yellow tape where the man's body was covered. "I've never seen a dead body before, let's get closer," Ritchie urged.

"Okay," I agreed as we headed closer to the dead body that was sprawled out near a parked car. I heard of a few people getting killed in our projects, but like Ritchie I had never seen a dead body with my own eyes. The cops were talking amongst each other and to some residents. I figured they were trying to find witnesses, but I doubted anybody in our hood would say shit. I then noticed another man come up, but I figured he must've been a detective because he was wearing a suit. He went over to the body, bent down and lifted the sheet.

"Noooooooooooooo!" Is all I remember screaming out before running towards my dad's dead body.

"Nico, come back," I heard Ritchie yell out, but I was gone.

"He can't be dead! My dad can't be dead," I kept screaming trying to reach him, but was held back by one of the officers. "Let me go! Let me go! I have to get to my father!"

I could hear voices talking to me, but I couldn't understand their words. I had zoned out. My mind was in another place. The man that I had looked up to and wanted to be like, was gone. Someone had put a bullet through his head and left him bloodied on the concrete like he was trash. My father was dead.

For the next few weeks after my father died, I refused to come out of my room. The only place I went was to his funeral. The pain I was in seemed almost unbearable. I was full of rage. I wasn't sure if I was angry because I blamed my father for leaving me. Although I knew somebody shot and killed him, I still felt like it was his fault.

"Nico, unlock the door!" I heard my mother scream, interrupting my thoughts.

I got up from the bed and took my time unlocking the door, not wanting to be bothered.

"Boy, you need to get yo' shit together. You can't just stay in this damn room every day all day. You need to take yo' ass back to school," she belted, looking around my bedroom.

"I don't feel like going to school. I just want to stay in my room," I said, lying back down on my bed.

"I don't give a damn what you feel like doing. Yo' father is dead, now get over it," she said and slammed the door.

I wanted to bury my face in the pillow and cry, but I was tired of crying. It wasn't going to bring my father back. So instead of crying I started punching my pillow. I needed to release all this anger I had balled up. I kept punching until I heard my mom calling my name.

"Nico, come here. Somebody is here to see you."

At first I wasn't going to come out my room because I figured it was Ritchie or one of the other kids in the neighborhood, but I decided to see; because honestly my frustrations were getting the best of me and I felt like I was suffocating. I needed to breathe.

"There's my guy," I heard a cheerful voice say when I walked out of my bedroom.

"Uncle Marvin, it's good to see you," I said with a slight smile when I saw his tall slim body, dressed in his standard attire of a suit, standing by the door.

"It's good to see you, too," he said, giving me a hug. "Listen, I wanted you to go for a ride with me. That is if your mother doesn't mind," he said, looking over at my mom.

"Go 'head. If you can get him out his room and this apartment then by all means take him," she said huffing.

"How 'bout it, Nico?" Marvin questioned.

"Sure," I said somewhat reluctantly. "Give me a minute. I need to get dressed."

"Take your time. I'll be right here waiting for you."

By the time I took a shower and got dressed I was actually ready to go and looked forward to spending some time with Uncle Marvin. He was almost like the closest person I could get to that was like my dad. They had known each other since before I was born and were so tight that they had a lot of the same body gestures and similar word usage.

"I heard you weren't doing too well," Uncle Marvin said when we got in his car. "I miss your dad, too," he added.

"Why did God have to take my dad from me? I just don't understand. He was the only person that loved me," I said, putting my head down.

"That's not true, Nico. I love you, your mom love you, and so does Chrissy."

I looked up at Uncle Marvin and could see the sincerity in his eyes, but I wasn't all the way convinced about my mother. I didn't tell him that though. I knew he meant well and I figured that's what really mattered.

"I don't know what to do now that he's not here anymore," I confided.

"You stand up and be the young man he taught you to be. Your father was strong and he raised you to be the same way. I can't never replace your father, but I'll step in where he left off, if you want me to."

"You mean I can still come hang out at your store and stuff?"

"All that. We can go to the games, you can help me run errands, I'll get your school clothes or whatever you need, I got you. Your father looked out and came through for me more times than I can count and I know he would want me to come through for you."

"Thank you, Uncle Marvin," I said, genuinely grateful that I still had him in my life.

"You don't have to thank me. I feel honored. You know you've always been like the son I never had. You will get through this. We both will. There is somebody who wants to see you if you're up to it."

"Who?" I wanted to know.

"Chrissy. She's been asking about you, but she didn't feel comfortable calling over to your mother's house."

"Yes, I do miss Chrissy."

"Great. She gonna be happy to see you. Don't ever think you're alone in this. We're here for you Nico," Uncle Marvin reassured me as we headed to Chrissy's place.

I sat back in the car and for the first time since my father died, I felt a glimpse of hope. I would never get over losing my dad, but I didn't feel so alone anymore. Being around my mother, she didn't seem to understand or care about my pain, but now I felt like I had other people I could share my sadness with. I finally believed that I would get through the darkest days of my life.

Chapter 4

It's My Time

It had been over a year since my father was murdered and not a day went by that I didn't think about him. There had been no arrest, but I continued to keep my ears to the street believing that one day I would find out exactly who was responsible for his death. In the meantime, I continued to become more immersed in learning the game and the more time I spent with Uncle Marvin, the more that became true. Unlike my father, Uncle Marvin wasn't constantly preaching to me about doing well in school and going to college. He seemed to actually enjoy the act of hustling unlike my dad.

See, my dad looked at selling drugs as a way to make money and take care of himself and his family.

He didn't have a high school degree and felt there wasn't a legitimate way of making enough money to provide for his family sufficiently. That's why my dad always stressed the importance of me going to school because he didn't want me to have to hustle like he did. The thing was, I honestly got some sort of excitement from learning how the drug game worked. To me, it equated to being your own boss and running a corporation if you played your cards right. Uncle Marvin saw that hunger in me and fed it every chance he got.

"Uncle Marvin, I was thinking," I said casually as we were in his store unpacking boxes of cigarettes.

"Should I be worried? I know what happens when you get to thinking," he joked.

"Nah, you don't have to be worried. I think it will help you out."

"Then get to talkin'," he said enthusiastically.

"I'm always hearing you complain about how Corey is running the project across from where I live."

"Yeah... and?"

"Well, the only reason you keep him is because you don't have anybody else you trust that knows them blocks."

"True, so what's your point?"

"I can oversee that project. I know those blocks like the back of my hand."

"Boy, I ain't got time to be entertaining your

jokes right now." Uncle Marvin chuckled brushing me off.

"I'm not joking. Like I said, I know the blocks, you can trust me and I'll bust my ass to make sure that project turns into a goldmine for you," I said confidently.

"You serious?" He said, stopping in the middle of lifting a box and staring at me.

"You know I don't joke when it comes to business."

"You sounded just like your father when you said that." Uncle Marvin grinned.

"So does that mean yes?"

"Nope."

"Why?"

"You not ready yet plus you got school."

"We get out next week. That would be the perfect time for me to grind and really get my hands dirty. Think of it as my job for the summer."

"I tell you what. I'll tell Corey that I want you to work for him for the summer."

"Why I gotta work for that chump?" I questioned, feeling like working for Corey was beneath me. From what I heard he was lazy and did a half ass job when it came to running those corners. Instead of bringing in the profits it had the potential to make, he would basically break even.

"Hold up. Let me finish," Uncle Marvin said, putting up his hand. "One thing you'll learn about running a business is: A) never get rid of a worker until you've gotten everything you need from them and they're no longer a benefit, and B) if at all possible don't let a worker become an enemy unless you prepared to kill him."

"How is Corey's lazy ass a benefit?" I was curious to know.

"Mainly because if he sees you as working for him, he'll say and do things that can enhance your skills if you take over. Meaning that, the bullshit he does that hinders his ability to make money, you'll see it and you'll know not to do that same dumb shit. And the decisions he makes that are profitable, I don't care if it's only a handful, you take those business skills and you apply them to make sure you run your operation even tighter."

"I get what you're saying. I only have one thing to add."

"What's that?"

"It's not *if* I take over it's *when* I take over, because you will want me to take over. These streets will be mine. You wait and see." I smiled.

"You too much, Nico. All I can say is I'm glad you on my side." Uncle Marvin laughed.

For the last few weeks I felt like I had become Corey's personal do boy. That nigga was bossing me around like I was on his payroll although he wasn't giving me a dime; my money came straight from Uncle Marvin. I played my position though. Corey had no idea that everyday I was waiting and plotting on taking over his spot.

"Corey, after I drop this package off, I'ma head home. I'll be back first thing in the morning," I said, before jumping off the top of the stairs.

"That ain't gon' work. I need you to come right back. I have somewhere I need to go so I need you to hold shit down while I'm gone."

"But you just got back from being gone for like two hours," I said, frowning at his clown ass.

"What, you clockin' my time now? You work for me, not the other way around, motherfucker." I walked back over to Corey and we were standing eye to eye. Although he was five years older than me I was tall for my age so we were the same height. I started to ball up my fist because I was about to punch him dead in his mouth, but I caught myself. My father had always told me the importance of keeping your emotions in check, especially when you were anger, so I stepped back.

"My fault, Corey. You right... I work for you."

"Exactly," he shot back like he was the boss of some shit. But that's what I wanted him to think.

"No disrespect. I'll drop this off and I'll come right back. You go and handle whatever you need to and I'll hold it down this way."

"Now that's the attitude I'm talkin' 'bout. You

act right I might let you leave the block a little early tomorrow. Now hurry up 'cause I got a piece of ass waitin' on me," Corey boasted.

I simply nodded my head like the obedient motherfucker Corey wanted me to be. As I walked to my destination I kept replaying the bullshit conversation I had with my so-called boss. It had only been a few short weeks since Uncle Marvin sent me in to prove myself and business had already improved drastically and it had nothing to do with Corey. He was even a lazier fuck than I thought he was. Not only that, he got off on treating me like a minion. Letting me do all the work but he take all the credit. But Corey would get his and never see it coming.

"I don't ever see you no more," Ritchie said while we sat in my room watching television.

"I'm out here hustlin' man. If I'm hangin' wit' you that mean I ain't makin' no money." I chuckled.

"What about school? Once the summer break ended, you came for the first couple weeks and then you started disappearing. It seems like you coming less and less. Your mother cool with that?"

"She don't know. I be intercepting the letters from the school and deleting the messages they leave on the answering machine. Plus, it ain't like I've completely dropped out." I shrugged.

"At the rate you going, it's close to it."

"School ain't for everybody. We all have a gift and mine can't be found between the pages of a book. My gift is knowing how to make money on these streets. Uncle Marvin said at my age now, I'm just as sharp as my dad was when he was running the blocks. Can you believe that," I said wide eyed.

"Foreal!" Ritchie said as if he was impressed by what I said.

"Yep. But I'ma be even sharper than my dad. He got caught slippin' in these streets and it cost him his life. After all this time we still ain't found his killer," I said, shaking my head. "But one thing I've learned is you can't trust nobody. It's a jungle out here. These niggas are animals."

"You can trust me," Ritchie replied with his puppy dog eyes staring up at me.

"I know man," I said rubbing his head playfully. "You haven't been corrupted by this game so you don't count. You still green." I laughed.

"Stop making fun of me. I bet I could be a good worker, too."

I kept laughing at Ritchie until I realized he was serious. "What, you want to join me on the block... is that what you saying?"

"Yeah, why not?"

"Ummm, weren't you screaming books and shit, schoolboy. You can't be on the corner hustlin' if you stuck in school."

"I can work after school and on the weekends."

"Ritchie, I don't think you cut out for this shit."

"You forget my dad used to hustle with your dad, so I bet I would be good at it, too. Just give me a chance," Ritchie said.

"Why, the sudden interest?"

"Because I miss hanging out with my best friend," Ritchie said sincerely.

"Listen, some things are about to change soon. The dude Corey who is overseeing things is on his way out and I'll be taking over."

"Foreal? You gonna be the man over them projects?" Ritchie asked with excitement.

"Sure am. And when that happens, I'ma need some trustworthy soldiers under me and you'll be my first recruit."

"You mean that, Nico?"

"I said it didn't I? I give you my word on that. Just be patient and give me a little time," I said nodding my head. I was serious, too. My conversation with Ritchie got my hustlin' juices flowing. I had been focusing so much on knocking Corey out the picture that I hadn't thought about what I would do once I did. I needed to start compiling my team of who would follow me and Ritchie was first on my list. He was leaned more on the soft side, but Ritchie was loyal, followed directions and was a good listener. Those were key qualities to be a suitable member of my team. If everything continued

to come together correctly, I would be able to takeover even sooner than I had anticipated.

Chapter 5

The Devil Is A Lie

"I thought you said you were staying over Ritchie's house tonight?" my mom said when I walked through the door.

"It's good to see you too, Ma," I shot back, not up for a conversation after working the block all damn day.

"What you came to get something before you leave?" she continued.

"No. I'm not staying at Ritchie's tonight. I'm tired. All I want to do is go to sleep in my own bed," I explained.

"Well, if you staying here you gon' have to stay in your room because I'm tired too and I don't want to be disturbed. That means none of yo' friends can come over either," my mom added.

"Whatever," I mumbled under my breath before going in my room and closing the door. I was exhausted and didn't even care why my mom was running her mouth. I was used to her talking crazy so I didn't even ask her any questions. Plus, I had no desire to have company or come out my room. The block was on fire all day and night so the only thing I wanted was some sleep. Before my head even hit the pillow it was lights out for me. I fell into a deep sleep and didn't awake until the middle of the night when I needed to use the bathroom. I was sleeping so good that at first I fought off the urge to get up, but eventually I gave in.

When I opened my bedroom door I stopped in my tracks because I heard arguing. But it wasn't the loud voices that made me pause, it was who they were arguing about that made me take a closer listen. I stepped in the hallway making sure not to make a sound. I quietly walked towards the living room so I could hear even better. I was tempted to peep my head around the corner so I could see who my mother was arguing with, but I decided not to take the chance, because I definitely didn't want to be seen. I was able to catch all the dialogue and that's what mattered most at this point.

"I ain't heard nothing from you in over a year and you call me out the blue yesterday saying you want to see me. I'm thinking you finally got some money for me, but you show up here empty handed. What type of shit is that!"

"Shaniece, calm yo' ass down. You know shit was hot for me after Royce got killed. I had to get outta town."

"Oh please! Didn't nobody know you had anything to do with his murder. You just didn't keep yo' end of the bargain that's why yo' ass bounced. I did my part now it's time for you to pay up."

"I told you he didn't have no money on him."

"Tyrone, you a lie! I know for a fact he had just dropped off a package to Jerome and picked up a lot of money."

"Well, like I told you that day he ain't have it on him. I don't know who got the money, but it wasn't me."

"After all this time you still sticking to that damn story?"

"Cause it ain't no story, it's the truth."

"So basically you saying that I set up Royce to be killed for nothing. Ain't that some bullshit!"

It felt as if someone had pounded me in the head with a hammer and wouldn't stop. I leaned up against the wall to regain my composure. I couldn't wrap my mind around what I had just overheard. My mother was responsible for my father's death. My emotions were on overdrive and I felt at any moment I might explode, but I knew that would be the wrong move. I had to keep my cool, but I also had to see the person that pulled the trigger and killed my father.

"Nico, what are you doing up?" my mother snapped when I came walking in the living room

"I wanted to get some juice from the kitchen," I mumbled, rubbing my eyes as if I had just woken up.

"Well hurry up!" she snarled with her arms folded.

I walked slowly, trying to pretend that I wasn't paying attention to the man sitting on the couch. He had his head tilted down as I strolled passed him. There was an eerie silence while I poured some juice. Neither my mother nor the man said a word the entire time I was in the kitchen. When I finished drinking the juice I put the glass in the sink before coming out. That's when it happened. It was as if I caught the man off guard and our eyes met. They locked for what felt like an eternity. I could tell my glare was making the man uneasy, but I didn't care. I wanted to remember every detail, from his haircut, the shape of his eyes, the color of his skin and every feature on his smug face.

"Is there a problem lil' homey?" the man finally said, tired of me burning a hole through him with my glare.

"Nah, just wanted to see who was keeping my mom company in the middle of the night."

"That ain't none of yo' business, Nico. Now take yo' ass back to bed!" my mom shouted.

I simply nodded my head and went to my room. I locked the door and for a few minutes I stood there with my fist balled up. My breathing became rapid and I wasn't sure what to do to calm myself, but the thing was I didn't want to get calm. I wanted to stay angry and enraged so that's what I did. I sat on the edge of my bed and remained up for the rest of the night plotting and planning my next move.

The next day after I overheard the conversation between my mother and Tyrone I began asking around to see if anybody knew who he was. Luckily, he was a local dude that had been a low level dealer in the neighborhood. I found out where he hung out and for the next few weeks I began tracking his moves. I had become consumed with clocking every step he made that I had to tell Uncle Marvin I needed to take a break from working the blocks. I lied and told him my mother found out I wasn't going to school and so I needed to buckle down on my studies before I flunked out. He understood and said my job would be waiting for me whenever I was ready to come back. I did plan on going back to the block, but for now Tyrone was my top priority.

I watched from a short distance as Tyrone kicked it with a few guys in front of a corner store. After smoking a cigarette, he headed up the street and I figured he was on his way to see this chick I found out he was fucking with. He seemed to go visit her almost every other day, but tonight's visit would end much different.

Like clockwork, Tyrone came sauntering out of the chick's crib a couple hours later and then took the same backstreet shortcut he always used. He was so busy smoking that Tyrone didn't notice I was on his ass until he felt the tip of cold metal against the back of his head.

"Yo... yo... yo... what the fuck!" Tyrone said, putting his hands up. "I ain't got shit on me."

"Nigga, don't nobody wanna rob you. That's what yo' pussy ass like to do. Now keep walking," I directed, nudging the gun even harder against his head, leading him towards a back alley.

"Where we going?" he asked nervously.

"Just move!" I yelled. Tyrone was actually a little nigga so I was tempted to pick his ass up and throw him in the alley, but I started pushing him instead. I had replayed this moment so many times in my head that I was eager to see it through once and for all.

Once we reached the alley, I shoved Tyrone down causing him to knock over one of the trashcans. I could have easily killed Tyrone when I first walked up on him from behind, but I wanted him to see my face before he died. "Remember me, motherfucker," I said aiming the gun at his face.

Tyrone frowned at me with a raised eyebrow

not saying a word. He kept staring at me as if trying to place where he recognized me. "Am I supposed to?"

"So you wanna act like you don't know. Let me help..."

"Wait, you Shaniece son," he said cutting me off. "Hold up. Did yo' mom put you up to this? Let me explain," he stuttered.

"I don't need you to explain shit. I already know everything. I heard the conversation between you and my mom. I know it was you that killed my father."

"You got it all wrong. It was all your mother's idea. I was only tryna help her out. She said he was beatin' her and shit," he rambled.

"Shut the fuck up!" I barked, anxious to pull the trigger. "I know my mother had you rob and kill my father and you gon' die for that shit."

"Wait... wait... wait. I got some money at my crib. I can give it to you," he tried to reason.

"I don't want nothing from you but yo' life. You killed my father and the only thing that gives me a little peace of mind is that your blood is on my hands. Now die nigga." Before Tyrone could say another word I lit his body up emptying the entire chamber in his face and chest. His brain splatter covered the brick wall as Tyrone's body slumped down to the ground. At the age of 14, I could now add killer to my resume.

Chapter 6

On My Own

"Nico, where do you think you going?" my mother questioned, as I stood in front of the door with a large duffel bag in my hand.

"I'm leaving. I can't stay here no more."

"Boy, what is you talkin' 'bout."

"I can't stay in the same place with you for one more day. Having to look at your face right now is making me sick."

"Who in the hell do you think you talkin' to! You betta watch yo' mouth before I knock yo' teeth out," my mother threatened, stepping towards me.

"I'm talkin' to you and I advise you not to step any closer," I warned. My mother's eyes widened in rage and her nose began to flare like it would when she was about to lose it. She lounged at me and I grabbed her wrist midair. Her anger had now switched to being stunned. "You will never put your hands on me again," I stated still holding on to her wrist.

"You done lost your motherfuckin' mind!" she screamed before lounging her other arm at me, but I dropped my duffel bag and held her other wrist too. I was tall and towered over my mother. I could've easily broken both her wrist and she knew it.

"Step away from me," I said coldly, before releasing her from my grasp. The look in my mother's eyes was a combination of shock, fury, and confusion.

"I don't know what the hell has gotten into you but..."

"Don't say another word," I said, putting my hand up. "I know what you did. It was you that set my father up to be killed. You!" I shouted so loudly I thought every piece of glass in the apartment would break. My mother began backing away from me as terror engulfed her face.

"Nico," she said in almost a whisper.

"You have never been a mother to me, but you had to take my father. If you hadn't given birth to me, you would be a dead woman right now."

"Son, you don't mean that."

"I'm not your son. You're nothing to me. I don't have a mother. Stay out my life. I don't ever want to see your face again."

"Nico, you don't mean that. You angry right now, but you have to understand. Your father wanted to take you away from me and raise you with his fiancé like she was yo' mother. I couldn't let that happen. I gave that man everything. I was good to yo' father, but instead of him appreciating it, he tossed me aside and wanted to take my only child. You have to understand, he left me no choice. I did it for you. Please forgive me," she pleaded.

"You didn't do it for me. You did it for yourself. It killed you that Daddy was happy and that even though he didn't want you, he loved me. You were jealous that I had a father that gave a fuck when you didn't. You gon' have to live wit' this shit for the rest of your pathetic life. But I won't be here to see it," I said, turning to leave.

"Nico, wait! Where will you go?"

"It don't matter. I'm dead to you," I said, shutting the door behind me.

When I showed up at Uncle Marvin's house with my duffel bag, instead of him grilling me, he showed me to his guest bedroom and told me I was welcome to stay for however long I wanted. He knew something was wrong and part of me wanted to tell him what had happened, but this other part of me wanted to protect my mother. I wanted nothing to do with her, but I also didn't want to be responsible for her death. I knew that Uncle Marvin would kill my mother himself if I told him the role she played in my father's death. I decided to let sleeping dogs lie as long as she stayed the hell out of my life.

"Uncle Marvin, listen I think I'm ready to take over for Corey," I said casually as we sat in the kitchen eating breakfast.

"Really now," he replied, not looking up from the newspaper.

"Yep. I've been working with him for months and I'm basically maintaining the blocks. I know what to do to keep the money flowing," I said confidently.

"Umm hmm," he mumbled, taking a sip of his orange juice, but still not making eye contact with me.

"I've even began gathering my team to work the blocks with me." That got my uncle's attention because he finally looked giving me a curious glare.

"And who is going to be a part of your so-called team?"

"Ritchie is on board."

"You talking about Ricardo's son?"

"Yep, and my man Alton and Lance. I want to recruit two more guys, but I think that's enough to start with," I said, nodding my head like I had everything figured out.

"I see. I know Ritchie still in school what about Lance and Alton?"

"Lance is, but Alton graduated last year and right now he just working at this warehouse stocking boxes and stuff. He ready to get on these streets and make this money."

"I tell you what. If you get two more solid recruits then I'll let you take over for Corey."

"Foreal!" I couldn't contain my excitement. "You mean that, Uncle Marvin?"

"I do. But remember, you're vouching for your team so you're responsible for them. You get all the credit good or bad. So be wise with your decision-making process because your team will either make you or break you."

"Got you. But I promise I won't let you down. I'm gonna be the best that ever did it in these streets.

"So listen, I wanted us to meet up 'cause I had a conversation with my uncle earlier today and it's official."

"What's official?" Ritchie questioned like he was lost or some shit.

"I'm 'bout to take over them blocks and you all are gonna help me," I said without hesitation.

"Stop playing!"

"I ain't playin', Ritchie. I'm serious. I'm vouching for each of you so ya bet not let me down neither."

"We won't," Ritchie, Lance, and Alton said in unison.

"So when we start? I'm tired of stacking boxes for chump change. I need to make some real money," Alton huffed.

"There is only one... no, make that two hold-ups." I sighed.

"What's that?" Lance asked.

"I have to get two more solid guys to join our team before my uncle will let me take over for Co-rey."

"Nico, I got a cousin who would be perfect. He hungry like me, but he way smarter. I mean that nigga a math genius."

"Is he in school?"

"Nah."

"What he got a job... where he work?"

"That's the thing, he can't really keep a job. He was in school, but dropped out 'cause he was bored. Then he always get hired, but then he think he know more than his bosses, which he does, but they end up firing him 'cause he be telling them how they should do they job."

"I see," I said not feeling Alton's suggestion. The last thing I needed was a know-it-all telling me how to run my shit.

"It's like my auntie always saying, he too smart for his own good, but I do know he got nothing, but time on his hand and he will grind hard for you."

"I don't know, Alton. That motherfucker can't

be tryna tell me what the fuck to do. We a team, but I'm the leader of this team. He got to do what I tell him to do not the other way around."

"I feel you. At least meet him. I promise he's worth a meeting," Alton insisted.

"Okay, I'll meet him. Get him here tomorrow. I'm ready to get this shit rolling," I said, anxious to be rid of Corey. If Alton's cousin did work out then all I needed was one more person to set this shit off.

Chapter 7

Clique

"So you Reese," I said, sizing Alton's cousin up. "Alton, tells me you interested in being a part of the team."

"From what my cousin told me, it sounds like something I want to be a part of."

"Did Alton explain how this situation would work?" I wanted to know.

"What you mean?"

"Meaning, that although you would be a member of the team you would take orders from me. I heard you had a problem taking orders," I said, staring directly in his eyes. Reese shot a mean glare over to his cousin and Alton quickly put his head down like he got busted or something.

"I know how to take orders," Reese replied.

"I didn't say you don't know how to take orders, I said you have a problem taking orders, there's a difference. So will you have a problem taking orders from me?"

"Nah, I don't think I will."

"I don't need you to think, I need you to know. I'm a few years younger than you and Alton, but my father ran these streets. My uncle runs these streets and it's only right that I do it better than both of them. I say that so you understand that this is my shit. Nobody has ever or will ever do it better than what I'm about to do. Brooklyn and the surrounding boroughs will not only love me, but they'll respect me. That starts with my team. I don't need no on the fence niggas representing me."

"I wanna be a part of this and you the boss. I respect that," Reese said, standing up to shake my hand.

"Then you in my man," I said, shaking his hand. "We 'bout to do big things." I grinned, as Ritchie, Lance, Alton, and Reese all smiled. The excitement almost seemed contagious. I could feel the energy and it was getting me so hyped. All I needed was one more piece to the puzzle. I wanted it so bad I could almost taste the shit and it tasted even better than the sweet potato pie that Chrissy would bake. I just hoped to get my slice sooner rather than later.

As I stood on the corner watching Corey not doing shit, but laughing and joking, I wanted to smack that nigga. It had been a few weeks and I hit a snag in my operation. I couldn't find my fifth recruit for nothing. The other team members had brought person after person for me to meet, but none of them felt like the missing link instead more like dead weight. They didn't have that hunger in their eyes that for me was mandatory. My frustration level had reached a boiling point, but I had to keep my game face on while dealing with Corey. I didn't want him to have any idea that I was gunning for his position. But I couldn't front, the shit was working my patience. The nigga was a complete loser and taking orders from him was like a nonstop sucker punch.

"Nico, what you doing just standing there?" Corey barked, shaking me out of my thoughts. "We got work to do."

"I been working. All you gotta do is count that big knot in yo' pocket." I smirked.

"Well, you need to work harder. It's too much money out here to get. I gotta make a run so don't be slackin' off 'cause I won't be around to patrol you," Corey stated.

"You ain't neva around no way, so I'm good," I said under my breath.

"Speak up, I didn't hear you," Corey's punk ass said walking towards me.

"I said, I got you covered... you good."

"That's my nigga. I'll see you in a couple hours," he said, patting me on my shoulders like I was his pet dog or some shit.

Two hours passed and of course Corey was no-where in sight. He was probably running up in some dirty pussy since a fat ass always came before mon-ey with him. It began snowing and shit slowed all the way down. I was about to go inside one of the buildings when I saw a girl walking towards me. At first, I thought maybe it was a customer, but her eyes seemed too clear and alert to be an addict. *Maybe she making a buy for someone else,* I thought to myself.

"Are you Nico?" the cutie asked me. I didn't care how cute she was, I wasn't about to answer that question with a yes. This might be some type of set up.

"Nope."

"Do you know where I can find him?"

"Nope."

"Oh, well Lance told me he would be over here and I needed to speak to him."

"How you know Lance and what you need to speak to Nico about?"

"Lance dates my little cousin, Cheryl, and he said I might be able to get a job from Nico."

"A job? You wanna work for Nico?"

"Yep, why do you work for him?"

"I guess you can say that."

"How you like it?"

"It's cool, but he works the shit outta you. I mean, you see it's snowing out here and I'm still grinding. If you ain't willing to bust yo' ass then I would suggest you not even consider working for him. Just 'cause you a female he ain't gon' go no easier on you either."

"I wouldn't want him to. I would bust my ass just like a nigga would. I work at an after hours spot now and I bring in more money and work harder than any man in there."

"Then why you want to work for Nico?" I asked.

"'Cause they don't wanna pay me like they pay the men. Most of the time they don't want to pay me at all. They just use the women as eye candy to draw in customers, but I need money."

"Why, you got kids or something to take care of?"

"No. I'm just ready to get out of my mom's crib. She got a boyfriend and he always tryna have sex wit' me. I'm sick of fighting his ass off."

"Have you told your moms what's going on?"

"I'm too scared she'll throw me out if I tell her so I just wanna get my money up so I can leave on my own," she said shaking her head.

"What's your name?"

"Tracy... Tracy Taylor."

"So type of work you want to do for Nico?"

"As long as it don't require me to sell no pussy then I'll do whatever he wants," she said. And there it was, that hunger I was itching for. Even the snow couldn't hide the hunger in her eyes. Never did I think about recruiting a female to the team, but Tracy might be just what my clique needed.

"You got the job. Welcome to the team." I smiled.

"Don't I need to meet Nico first?"

"I am Nico."

"You're Nico! You had me running my mouth this entire time, thinking I was talking to one of Nico's workers and it was you. I feel like such a dumbass," Tracy said, putting her head down.

"You passed the test and you're in, so don't feel like a dumbass. You see how empty these streets are right now, but you out here in the snow begging for a job. That's the type of people I need out here representing me. You just might end up being my best worker."

"I will be your best worker. Thank you so much for the opportunity, you will not regret it."

"I know I won't. I'll have Lance get in touch with you when it's time to get started."

"When will that be because I really need to get to work."

"Sooner than you think." I smiled realizing that all of our lives were about to change forever.

Like the good do boy Corey thought I was, I waited for him to get back to the block five hours later and I handed him the rest of the money I earned. I gave him a fake ass smile and walked the fuck off. I knew his time was officially up so it was easy to play the bullshit game. I couldn't wait to get home and speak to Uncle Marvin. On the low, I think he started wondering if I was really going to be able to deliver and I wanted him to know that I had.

"Uncle Marvin, I'm so glad you here," I said as soon as I walked through the door.

"Where else would I be?" he laughed. "If I didn't know better, I would think you ran all the way home the way you huffing and puffing," he commented.

"Basically, I wanted to tell you the good news."

"What's that?"

"I found my fifth and final person. I finally got my team together," I announced proudly.

"Really? I know you were having some problems with that. It's been a few weeks now. So who is he?"

"It's not a he, it's a she."

"A she, meaning a female?"

"Yeah, her name is Tracy Taylor. But before you go passing judgment thinking a woman can't do the job, trust this one can," I said without hesitation.

"No judgment from me. Like I said, this is your team. You get the credit good or bad so if you want to vouch for this woman then that's on you."

"Thank you 'cause my instincts tell me she is going to be a great secret weapon in more ways than one."

"I see. Well, since you've held up to your end of the agreement then I'll deliver on mine. Just give me a week to handle the Corey situation."

"Uncle Marvin, let me handle it."

"I don't think you ready for that." Uncle Marvin grinned as if he found what I said funny.

"Trust me, I can handle it. Those are gonna be my blocks so let me deal with Corey."

"You sure?" Uncle Marvin questioned with caution.

"Positive. I'm about to be the boss of my team so I need to be able to make executive decisions, why not start with Corey?"

"Lead the way my boy. But if you change your mind and need my help just ask."

"I got this, but thanks." I smiled before heading to my bedroom.

I stayed up for the rest of the night getting my thoughts together. I was going to meet with my clique tomorrow and set shit in motion. There was no turning back now and I was ready for everything that would come my way.

Chapter 8

Crew Love

"This is our first official meeting as a crew. I believe each of you are going to play a vital role and I'm pleased to have you as a member of my team," I said, standing in front of Tracy, Ritchie, Alton, Lance, and Reese. They each sat looking up at me like they were war ready even Ritchie scary ass. I was impressed and excited at the same time.

"So, when we start working the blocks?" Alton was the first to ask.

"Yeah, cause I need to start making some coins, ASAP," Reese chimed in.

"Me too," Tracy added.

"I feel you. We all trying to get rich and I promise if each of you follow my lead, we will all make more money than we ever imagined," I promised.

"Foreal?" Ritchie asked, in his normal wide-eyed way.

"Yes, foreal, Ritchie, but we have to take care of one thing first."

"What is it? Let's get it done so we can start making that money," Lance said, as everyone nodded their head in agreement.

"I need to get rid of Corey and Tracy I need your help to do it."

"Tell me what I need to do."

"I need you to put on your tightest best fitting jeans and take a walk down the block where we hustle at."

"Wait, you don't want me to fuck this nigga do you?" she questioned.

"Nope, you won't have to. I just need you to be the perfect bait. No disrespect, you have a fat ass and a pretty face so you are the perfect bait," I explained.

"So, what's the rest of the plan?" Tracy wanted to know.

"After you come walking down the block, when he approaches you, give him your digits. Wait for him to call and when he does I'll tell you what to do next because I'll take it from there."

"What if he doesn't try to holla?" Tracy asked.

"Ass is Corey's weakness so best believe he will try to holla. Just make sure you don't have on a coat that's covering yo' ass up when you take that walk." I smiled.

"Got you. So when do you want me to do it?"

"Tomorrow. I'll call you in the morning to let you know the exact time, so be waiting by your phone."

"Nico, man what you gon' do to Corey?" Lance asked.

"What you think... I'ma get rid of his motherfuckin' ass."

"Like kill him?" Ritchie questioned, looking scared.

"Yeah, nigga. He's a problem that needs to be erased. If I let him live, trust he'll come back for retaliation. We can't leave no loose ends."

"Nico, you the man!" Lance jumped up and said, shaking my hand.

"I'm not the man yet, but I will be," I said, nodding my head confidently. "A'ight ya, this meeting is over. We'll start working on Friday if everything goes as planned and I have no doubt that it will."

It was cold as a motherfucker outside but the sun was shining bright, just the way I liked. I stood on the stool kicking shit with Corey, something I normally didn't do, but I needed to hype his ass up for what was about to go down.

"Damn, look at shorty coming up the street," I commented as if I was about to holla at a girl. "She pretty as hell," I said as Tracy made her approach right on cue.

"Yeah, she cute, but what that ass looking like?" Corey huffed, nonchalantly.

"I don't know, but she bad and I'm 'bout to get them digits," I said, standing up as if I was about to walk off.

"Hold up youngin'," Corey said, placing his hand on my coat right as Tracy was slowly walking past us. She was on point with the shit too. Them jeans were gripping her ass and she was wearing a cropped jacket that was accentuating every curve she had. Even in the freezing cold I could tell Corey was like a dog in heat. "That's way too much woman for you, young homey. You sit yo' ass down and let a real man handle this," Corey boasted.

I pretended to feel some kinda way as he pimp walked over to Tracy. I could tell that at first she tried to act like she wasn't interested and let Corey continue to spit game. A few minutes later he was grinning and I knew that meant he got the number. Shortly after, Corey came back over to the stool where I was grinning from ear to ear.

"See, that's how you handle business. Watch, I'll be all up in that pussy by tomorrow," Corey bragged.

"You think so? Homegirl bad. She might try to play hard to get."

"Fuck that, I buy her a meal, spit a lil' game, and them panties coming off."

"You sound awfully sure."

"'Cause I am. Don't no chick tell me no."

"So sure you wanna place a bet?" I said, getting Corey hyped up.

"Oh, so just wanna giveaway yo' money. Sure, I'll be more than happy to take yo' chump change. I'll use it to pay for the next bitch meal I buy."

"Let's put a hundred on it then."

"Have my money first thing Thursday, 'cause like I said I'll be all up in them ovaries tomorrow night." Corey laughed. "But enough of all this bullshitting. Get back on them blocks and make me some money," he ordered.

"Whatever you say, boss." I gave a sly smile and went to work.

I spent the rest of the day laughing to myself about Corey. His arrogance would be the death of him literally.

"I'm a little nervous," Tracy said when I met her at her house that night. "I wasn't expecting him to call so soon."

"I did place a bet with him to make sure there were no delays," I admitted.

"A bet... like for money?"

"Yeah, I had to speed shit up. Aren't you ready to get to work?"

"You know I am, but I've never set nobody up to be killed before," Tracy said, seeming uneasy.

"Before I hired you, you said you were willing to do anything for the job except sell pussy. Are you backing out now?"

"Hell no! I said I was nervous, I didn't say I wouldn't do it. I'm a woman of my word and I need this job."

"Then you betta put on your best poker face. You can't be acting nervous and shit around Corey. You don't want to raise any suspicions," I said.

"I'll be ready for tomorrow, I promise," Tracy said.

"Remember, during dinner you have to drop subtle hints that you down to drop them panties for him. If he ask to come to your place tell him he can't 'cause yo' mom is home and she don't allow you to have guys over. That's when he should invite you to this apartment he keeps in Brooklyn where he take all his chicks to fuck."

"Then what?"

"I'll be waiting. You just keep your cool. That's the most important thing."

"You don't have any sort of fear about killing someone or that the table can turn and Corey can end up killing you?" Tracy asked me with a confused looked on her face.

"I used to fear my father, but he's no longer here. So now, I fear nobody, but God. Only He can judge me and when my time comes I'll take whatever punishment He sees fit. But while I'm here in these streets I'ma do whatever I need to survive and for me, survive means to win. Everyday I'm taking a chance with my life, but I'll take the risk," I said matter of factly.

"Nico, I don't understand how you are so young, but so focused and driven. Where does that come from?"

"Pain. It can either break you or make you. I use my pain as ammunition to become unstoppable."

"I'm just happy you letting me come along for the ride." Tracy smiled. "Because there is no doubt that whatever you put your mind to, you will make happen."

"Long as you know. So be ready 'cause this ride is gon' have a lot of twist and turns. Don't say I didn't warn you. But let me get outta here. You have a big day ahead of you tomorrow so I want you to get your mind right," I said before opening the front door.

"Don't worry, Nico, I won't let you down. I wanna see you become the King of New York." Tracy winked her eye.

"Have a goodnight," I said and closed the door. I stood in the hallway for a second thinking about the King of New York statement Tracy made. I wanted that too and was willing to do just about anything to make it happen.

Chapter 9

Takeover

The apartment Corey kept was a walkup in a seedy part of Brooklyn. The front door entrance lock didn't even work properly, so it was nothing for me to get inside and post up. The rent was stabilized and most of the tenants were older and had been living there the majority of their lives. For that reason, I didn't have to worry about being seen because there wasn't any heavy foot traffic coming in and out. It was the perfect spot for a cheap, dirty nigga like Corey to do his shit.

I got to the location early because I wanted to have plenty of time to get my own mind right. Although I had told Tracy to do that, I needed to do the same thing. Yeah, I had already killed one person, but that was different. I was driven by rage and revenge for my father. Corey's death was more of a business decision. Nah, I didn't like the silly fuck, but I didn't dislike him enough to want him dead. But from a business standpoint, I knew if I let him live I would always be looking over my shoulders, wondering not if, but when he would come back to take what he felt was stolen from him... his blocks. The time, energy and work it would take for me to become a boss would bring enough headaches; I could not let Corey be an unnecessary one.

As I began thinking about all the moves me and my crew would make and the plans I had for us I heard the entrance door open. I had already scoped out the area ahead of time and knew Corey's apartment was on the second floor. I told Tracy when they walked through the door for her to start laughing and talking a little loud so I would know it was them and get into position. At first I didn't hear anything, but when I stepped closer to the stairwell I heard a female giggling.

"Corey, you so silly," Tracy said extra loud and giggled some more.

"Shhh, shhh, keep yo' voice down, baby. Ain't nothing, but senior citizens up in here. We don't wanna wake them up." Corey's corny ass chuckled.

"You right." Tracy giggled again. "I can't wait for us to get some alone time," I heard Tracy say as they began to walk up the stairs.

"Me too, wit' yo' fine self," I heard Corey say

then it sounded like he smacked Tracy's ass.

"Boy, you so silly," Tracy said making eye contact with me as they were about to turn the corner. Corey hadn't noticed me yet because his eyes were still glued to Tracey's ass, but once they reached the hallway midway I stepped out of the darkness.

"Nigga, what the fuck is you doing here," Corey barked, but kept walking towards me.

"Baby, who is this?" Tracy questioned, pretending to be as shocked as Corey was by my presence.

"Nobody. He just a lil' nigga that work for me. He must got some money for me or something," Corey said to Tracy before turning his attention back to me. "Is that why you here, to bring me some damn money? It better be a lot since you decided to interrupt my evening wit' my baby," Corey said, trying to show off in front of his date.

"My man, Corey. I just wanted to come over and tell you bye." I gave him a half smile and he raised his eyebrow with a puzzled look on his face. Before any more words could be spoken, I fired off three bullets in his chest and one in his face just to make sure he was dead. Tracy covered her mouth to stop from screaming. I quickly grabbed her arm so we could get the fuck outta there before someone decided to open their door to see where the noise was coming from. But more than likely, they slept right through the shit and wouldn't notice Corey's dead body until the morning.

"Damn, Nico! You said we would start work on Friday and here we are. I wasn't sure if you would be able to make that happen, but now I know not to ever doubt you again," Alton said, cheesing extra hard.

"I try to be a man of my word." Although I had just turned 16, I did feel like a man. As I began my rise to the top, I did want a reputation as being a man of my word and that started with my own team. I planned to lead by example.

Friday came around fast so I created a preliminary schedule to see who worked best together. Since Alton and Reese were out of school they both worked the morning shift. I started them off together to see if they would develop a healthy competition since they were cousins. Or if it would have the opposite effect and they would be too lax because they spent the majority of the time kicking it instead of working. Since Tracy was also not in school I planned on having her switch up and work with Alton and Reese separately to see how she vibed with each of them and also with Lance and Ritchie. Since Lance and Ritchie were both still in school they would work mostly on the weekends and in the evening time after school. Adjustments would be made accordingly, but I thought this was a decent start.

"So listen, I'ma spend this weekend working with both of you. I want you to watch and learn. Monday, you'll work the blocks without me, so I can see what you can do. Got it?" I asked looking Alton and Reese in their eyes.

"Yep," they said in unison nodding their heads.

"When Tracy, Lance, and Ritchie come later on then the two of you will be dismissed from your shift. So let's get started," I said ready to get to work.

"I'm ready," Alton spoke up extra giddy.

"Me too," Reese added.

The day seemed to go by quick as hell, mainly because the blocks were on fire. The cold weather was starting to break so the fiends were out like cockroaches. Alton and Reese was on it too. They didn't let a customer get away. When their shift was over and Tracy, Lance, and Ritchie came they still didn't leave. Although I told them they wouldn't get paid for the overtime they still stayed because they said they wanted to continue to watch and learn. That was their first test and they passed it. If Alton and Reese were anxious to get off the block just because they weren't getting paid, then I knew they weren't the soldiers I needed to take me to the level I planned to go. My entire crew and me hustled those blocks together until we fed every last customer and shut the streets down.

Chapter 10

Spread My Wings

"Damn, what the fuck is you putting in that crack? Ya making a killing out there." Uncle Marvin shook his head as he counted the money I made for him that day. "Every week the profit keeps increasing."

"I told you I wouldn't let you down, Uncle Marvin."

"Hell, if I knew you would be flipping money like this, I would've gotten rid of Corey a long time ago."

"Maybe now you'll never sleep on me again." I shrugged.

"Boy, I'm scared of you."

"Stop playing, Uncle Marvin." I chuckled.

"I ain't playing. Boy, you dangerous. You done

taken a group of knuckleheads and turned them into moneymakers. Do you know what sort of leadership skills a man has to possess to pull something like that off?" my uncle said as if amazed.

"My crew ain't knuckleheads," I said, feeling some type of way about that jab.

"Don't take it as an insult to your crew, Nico. Take it as my admiration for you. Them folks didn't know nothing about selling no dope until they started fuckin' wit' you. I'ma be honest. I didn't think the shit was gon' work. But like I always teach you, be a man of your word and so I wanted to keep mine. You have proved me wrong all the way and honestly, I'm proud of you. Now I see why your father always wanted you to stay in school and go to college, 'cause you smart as a whip."

"You know how much I love and miss my father, but school was never my thing. It couldn't hold my attention, but hustling these streets do. I just hope my father ain't looking down on me disappointed," I said somberly.

"Let me tell you something, Nico. Your father loved you more than anything on this earth. You getting up everyday and grinding for yours. It may not be the way your father would've preferred, but you can't never be disappointed in a man that works for his. So get that bullshit out your head. You hear me?"

"Yes, I do, and thanks for saying it."

"Shiiit, thanks for all this money you making

me. Here's your cut and a little extra."

"That's what's up, Uncle Marvin," I said, taking the money with a huge smile on my face.

"Also, I know I never mentioned this, but I respect how you handled that Corey situation. You got a lot of balls. I be forgetting you only 16. You a bad boy. I wish you was my son."

"In a lot of ways I am," I said, giving Uncle Marvin a hug. "Now, let me get outta here. I got work to do." Uncle Marvin couldn't take the place of my father, but he was a great runner up. I had so much love for that man and it was mainly because he accepted me for who I was. He never tried to change me, but only kicked his knowledge and let me decide if and how I wanted to apply it. I respected that and respected him for it.

"Awww shit, we gettin' bonuses now!" Tracy popped, snapping her fingers and dancing.

"Good looking out." Ritchie grinned.

"Yeah, man, I appreciate it. You didn't have to do this," Lance added.

"You the best boss ever," Alton added.

"Most def appreciate it," Reese then said.

"Each of you have been puttin' in that work and I wanted to show my gratitude. This is only the beginning. In a couple months after we keep bringing in the profits, I'ma ask my uncle if we can expand," I said.

"What you mean expand?" Alton asked.

"That we not only work the blocks we have, but we run some more which will mean more money for us."

"You think your uncle will let that happen?" Ritchie wondered.

"My uncle is a businessman. If we keep bringing in those dollars then for sure. Why let someone else work a certain area if you have another team that can double or triple your profits," I said.

"Sounds about right to me. Plus, we have enough manpower and woman," Lance quickly added eyeing Tracy.

"Okay enough talking, time for work," I said, clapping my hands."

On the weekends business had gotten so crazy that I had all five of them working at the same time. It had actually been extremely beneficial. They had become so competitive with each other, but in a very good way. They also had each other's back. In the last few months we had become like a family. We hustled together, ate together, and hung out with each other. Because they had proven to be great workers I didn't have to be on the blocks as much. But instead of bullshitting with the extra time, I was putting it to good use by scoping out new opportunities to set up shop.

After I stayed on the blocks for a few with my crew I headed towards the train station to check out this spot I had been eyeing in East Flatbush. From what I heard, the previous crew that had been selling over there had got jammed up a few months ago and nobody had taken over since. For the last few weeks I had been going over there for a couple hours a day just checking out how shit was moving. I came to the conclusion, there was way too much money over on them block to be made and I couldn't let it go to waste. Now all I was trying to do was figure out the best way to have my team invade without it being hostile.

"Nico! Nico!" I heard someone calling out as I was headed to the train. I was so caught up in my thoughts that at first I didn't even hear them. When I turned around, I wished that I hadn't. "Nico, you didn't hear me calling you?"

"Nah... what do you want?"

"Does a mother need a reason to want to talk to her son," my mom said, standing in front of me. I hadn't seen her face since I walked out the apartment that day and I had no interest in seeing her now.

"We don't have nothing to talk about," I said point blank.

"I miss you, Nico. I thought you would've come home by now, but as the days and months passed I realized it wasn't gon' happen."

"Yep."

"You still mad at me?" she asked as if she had put me on a bullshit punishment for no reason and hoped I was over it.

"Mad? Mad doesn't begin to describe how I feel about you."

"I told you how sorry I was."

"Did you... if so I didn't care then and I still don't care now. I told you as far as I was concerned I no longer had a mother and I meant that. Ain't nothing changed. So if there's nothing else, I got a train to catch," I said ready to walk away.

"Nico, wait," she said taking my arm. "I ain't doing too good."

"That ain't my problem," I shot back pulling my arm away.

"You might hate me, but I'm still yo' mama. I heard you out here makin' money well I ain't got none."

"You shoulda thought about that before you had my father killed." My mom put her head down as if ashamed.

"I know I let you down and I'll never forgive myself for it. But please help me. I'm doing real bad, son." I glanced down at my mom and she did look like shit. I even wondered for a second was she using. She was always a petite woman, but now she was just skinny and her face seemed sunken in. She used to always keep her hair done, but now it was in a messy bun on top of her head. But no matter how bad she looked I felt absolutely zero sympathy for her.

"Take this," I said, handing my mom a wad of money. "I ain't giving you this because I want you back in my life. I'm giving you this money to make sure you stay out of it. This is the one and only time you'll ever get a dime from me, so don't come back," I said and walked away.

After scoping out the neighborhood in East Flat-bush for one more week, I was ready to bring my idea to Uncle Marvin. I was confident that my crew and I could handle the territory, now we would just need the additional product. Before I stepped to my uncle I wanted to make sure I could answer all the questions I knew he would throw my way. I was waiting patiently for him to come home, and when I heard the front door opening, I immediately turned off the television and stood up.

"What's up, Uncle Marvin!" I could feel myself smiling too hard. I couldn't front discussing new business excited me. Plus, this was the first time I was branching out and basically starting a project from scratch so I was extra excited.

"You seem like you're in an awfully good mood," my uncle said putting his keys down on the table.

"I am! I was waiting for you to get home because there was something I wanted to talk to you about," I said pacing back and forth.

"It's funny you say that because there was something I needed to talk to you about, too."

"Let me go first because I'm sure you gonna have a lot of questions," I said. My uncle simply nodded his head so I started running off at the mouth. "There is this neighborhood I've been eyeing for weeks. It's a new spot I want us to take over in East Flatbush. I know we can make a killing over there. My crew already has the current blocks in Bedford Stuyvesant on lock so we're more than capable of expanding. I was thinking of initially starting with Tracy, Lance, and Reese and then rotating with Ritchie and Alton once things get rolling. What you think?"

"Sounds like a plan and a good one," Uncle Marvin said casually.

"I'm glad you think so! I'm sure you have some questions so shoot," I said rubbing my hands together, prepared for whatever my uncle threw my way.

"I don't have any questions. I know what you're capable of and if you believe your crew is ready to expand then I say move forward."

"Really?" I had over prepared myself for this discussion with my uncle that I was disappointed he wasn't giving me the opportunity to put it on display.

"Is that all you wanted to talk to me about?

If so I wanted to have an important conversation with you."

"I'm finished. You have the floor," I said, wondering what was so important.

"I recently found out I have Stage IV lung cancer. I'm going to begin chemo treatments, but I'll be honest, Nico it's not looking good for me."

"What are you saying... are you gonna die?" I asked stunned by what my uncle said.

"We gon' all die, son but my death is coming a lot sooner than expected. I always thought the streets would kill me, not these damn cigarettes," he joked. "I've known something was wrong with me for awhile now, but I was in denial. I should've taken my ass to the doctor a long time ago."

"What will I do? You're all the family I have left."

"You have a family. Your crew is your family. You have Chrissy and don't forget about your mother."

"You're the closest person I have to my father left. Being around you makes me feel like he's still here with me," I revealed.

"Your father is with you. Right in here," Uncle Marvin said pointing at his chest. "Just like I will be too, when I pass away."

"You sound like you're giving up."

"Nah, I'ma give this a good fight. Hell, I might even whoop this cancer's ass, but I might not. Regardless, I want you to be prepared to carry on without me."

"This is too much," I said, shaking my head.

"I've said it before and I'll say it again... you a bad boy. You dangerous... you ahead of your time. These streets ain't ready for you. Don't you dare start getting scared now. You bet not let me down."

"I would never let you down, but I hate to do this without you."

"I felt the same way when Royce got killed, but I knew he would want me to carry on and you will do the same and I'm going to make sure of that."

"What you mean?"

"I've already told my plug about you, but I'm going to introduce you to him. He'll give you the product at the same price he's been giving it to me. I have already begun to let my buyers know that you will be their new supplier."

"Wait, you want me to takeover for you?"

"Of course. You've been groomed for this. Nobody can do this better than you and we both know it. I'm going to start treatment immediately so things will be rough on me pretty quickly. So get ready, you're the new boss," Uncle Marvin said shaking my hand. I shook his hand back, but I was still in shock. I always wanted to be the boss, but not like this, not because my uncle was sick. I was trying to take it all in stride, but it was difficult.

"I'll step up and do what I have to do to keep business going, but you'll beat this, Uncle Marvin. I know it. You'll beat this cancer and be back bossing everyone around in no time," I said giving him a hug.

Three months later Uncle Marvin died. Besides my father being murdered it was the saddest day of my life. But unlike then, I didn't stay in my room and mourn for weeks. Instead, I used the pain to grind even harder.

Chapter 11

Drug Dealer's Dream

5 Years Later...

"Happy Birthday, Nico Carter," the DJ blasted over the microphone as the club when crazy. I was celebrating my 21st birthday and I made sure to show out. I shut the club down and it belonged to me and my people for the night. I had champagne flowing, open bar, and everybody was partying like it was New Year's Eve in Times Square.

"Nico, this the best party ever, man!" Lance yelled, holding up his bottle of bubbly.

"He ain't lyin'!" Tracy said giving me a hug.

"You finally decided to show yo' ass up." I

laughed, hugging her back.

"Sorry 'bout that, but my girl here took forever to get dressed," Tracy said, nodding her head at the young lady behind her. I gave a quick glance to her friend and I couldn't help, but notice how pretty she was. I laughed to myself when I saw both Alton and Reese swooping in on her like hawks.

"No problem, just glad you made it. A party ain't a party without my number one girl." I smiled.

"I wouldn't have missed this party for nothing. Where Ritchie at?" Tracy asked looking around.

"He saw some girl in here he was checking for and went to talk to her."

"Oh yeah, there he is," Tracy said pointing at the bar across from our booth. "Ritchie stay whispering in some chicks ear." She giggled.

Tracy was right, Ritchie kept women in rotation. It was crazy because I still remembered Ritchie being the goofy, naïve teenager, but in the last few years after he started making real money and being in the streets all that shit changed. It's like he grew some balls and never looked back. But I was happy for my best friend. Although I thought he could slow down a tad on all the different females, I was happy he found his confidence and broke out of his shell because he damn sure was a late bloomer.

I couldn't help, but stand back, observe my crew, and smile. We had been going strong for years and now we were here tonight, celebrating my birthday, together as a family. They were all having a good time, laughing, smiling and our bond was stronger than ever. I knew both my dad and Uncle Marvin would be proud of what we had accomplished and me. We had managed to do what many would say was impossible in this game—stay alive, out of jail, and on top. That was because we always watched each other's back and stayed loyal not just to the game, but to our crew and it paid off. I had become one of the biggest players in these streets, moving more product than just about anybody. Things were going so well, we had begun expanding to Philly, Virginia, and North Carolina. I had become the epitome of a true boss and my drug dealer dreams were only beginning.

"Man, I can't believe after all that partying we did last night, you already up and out," Lance said, sounding like he was still sleep when I called him.

"Can't no business get done sleeping, nigga," I said getting out the car to hit up my favorite deli.

"You got me feeling like shit. Like I need to get my ass out of bed." Lance chuckled. "But then again, that's why you the boss. 'Cause while we sleepin' you up thinkin'."

"Pretty much, but don't forget Reese wanted us

to meet with a potential new buyer later on today."

"Damn, that shit is today. What time?"

"Five, you think you can have yo' lazy ass out the bed by then?" I joked.

"Yeah, I'll be up. Shiiit you done already fucked up my sleep. I'm 'bout to get up now. I'll hit you back when I hit the street."

"Cool," I said ending the call on my cell phone right as I stepped into the deli to get my favorite turkey bacon and egg sandwich. There was no need for me to place an order because soon as I walked through the door, they already knew what I wanted. I was what you would call a regular. After paying for my sandwich and orange juice, I was caught off guard when I turned around to leave.

"Hi, Nico," a vaguely familiar face said to me before I even made it to the exit door.

"Hey," I replied, trying to figure out where I recognized her face because I knew I had seen her before, but I couldn't place where.

"I guess you don't remember me. But that's not surprising since Tracy didn't introduce us."

"That's right. You're the girl that made Tracy late to my birthday party." I smiled.

"I'm sorry about that." She blushed. "I hope you don't hold it against me."

"No. I was just messing with you. So what's your name so I can call you something other than Tracy's girl."

"Angela, but everybody calls me Angie."

"So do you come to this deli often?"

"Not really, but I actually work in this office building around the corner."

"I guess it was a nice coincidence that we ran into each other."

"To be honest, it wasn't really a coincidence. I remembered a while ago when Tracy came to see me at work; she mentioned every morning you stopped by this deli around the corner from me. This is the only deli." Angela laughed nervously. "When I saw you yesterday at the club, I figured I take a chance to see if you were still coming here. I guess you are."

"Why didn't you introduce yourself yesterday at the party?"

"Nervous I guess. Then people kept coming up to you and I didn't want to be just another person you would forget."

"As pretty as your face is, I think you would be hard to forget. I mean, at first I couldn't remember where I had seen you, but it didn't take me long once you said Tracy's name. I see you're blushing again."

"Is it that obvious? Now I'm feeling embarrassed."

"Don't be embarrassed."

"I hope me showing up here doesn't make you think I'm some sort of stalker because I'm not... I promise." Angela giggled then gave me a cute smirk.

"I don't think you're a stalker. I actually respect the fact that you saw something you wanted and made a play for it."

"You make it sound like some sort of a game."

"Don't mind me, it's just how I talk. But listen, I have someplace I need to be."

"No, of course, I understand. I didn't mean to hold you up."

"I'm glad you did. Can I call you?"

"Of course," Angela said, writing her number down on a napkin before I could even pull out my cell phone. I found her eagerness cute and refreshing. Most of the women I came in contact with would be on some fake uppity shit, but be ready to fuck and suck the first night we went out. It was like they thought acting stuck up made them appealing, but all it did was make me want to dismiss they asses.

"I'ma call you. Maybe we can go out to dinner when you get off of work one day this week."

"I would love that."

"Cool, I'll call you tonight," I said walking off. "You really are pretty." I looked back and smiled. I could hear Angela giggling again and for the first that I could remember I was actually looking forward to our date.

By the time I finished running around and handling

most of my business it was almost five o'clock and time to meet up with Reese. At first I was tempted to postpone the meeting as I had a couple more things I needed to do, but I had already rescheduled two times before and I didn't want Reese to feel like I was giving him the runaround. Right when I was about to get on the bridge headed back to Brooklyn I saw Lance calling me.

"What's up, Lance?"

"I'm pulling up to the warehouse. Reese is already here and I'm guessing the other car is the guy we meeting with. You still coming right?"

"Man, you know I don't miss meetings. I am running late. I had a lot of shit to handle today. You go inside and talk to the dude. Give him our prices although I'm sure Reese already did and let them know I'll be there shortly."

"Will do. I see Tracy and Ritchie pulling in now too. I'll see you in a minute," Lance said before hanging up.

On my drive to the warehouse all I kept thinking was I hoped this dude Reese had us meeting wasn't a waste of my time. I spent each day wheeling and dealing for the next come up, I had zero time to waste. The only reason I was even entertaining dude was because Reese vouched for him and Reese was family, so I hoped he was the real deal.

Chapter 12

Nice To Meet You

"There's the man that makes everything happen," Alton said when I stepped in the warehouse.

"I was beginning to wonder if you was gon' make it," Reese added.

"My fault. Today was a lot more hectic than I anticipated. But I'm here now, let's get to it," I said walking over to where everyone was standing.

"Bink, this is Nico, Nico this is the new buyer I was telling you about." We shook hands and I was trying to size the dude up without seeming obvious.

"It's good to meet you, Bink. I know this was supposed to have happened awhile ago," I said upon releasing his hand.

"You a busy man and shit happens," Bink said

with ease. "Now that I finally have an opportunity to meet with you, I'm hoping we can do some business."

'That's the plan. Reese speaks highly of you and we all fam here so if the numbers make sense then I don't see why there would be a problem," I said getting a decent vibe from the dude.

"Like I was telling your partners, I have a huge crew in Upstate New York all they way on the other side of Maryland I have to feed. So we not talking small numbers. I have a large quantity of people I need to supply and if we can agree on a fair price I want you to be the sole distributor."

"I see." I glanced over at Lance and Ritchie who gave me the nod of approval. "Where's Tracy?" I asked wanting to get her input too. Although I could make or break any deals brought to the table, I preferred getting the okay from every member of my team so we were all in agreement. Before anyone could answer my question, Tracy came prancing out the back as if she heard me calling her name.

"There's my boo, what up, Nico." Tracy smiled. The sun hadn't even gone down and Tracy was already dressed to impress in her signature stiletto heels. She always had the appearance of a well-kept wife, little did people know she was lethal with a gun and would end your life without thinking twice. Besides me, Tracy was hands-down the best shooter in the crew.

"I was just asking about your whereabouts," I said.

"I had to freshen up in the bathroom. You know lady shit that ya don't know nothing about," she joked.

"Yeah, yeah, yeah... but um, Bink was telling me about the business he wanted to do with us."

"Yeah, I talked to him for a minute while we were waiting for the King's arrival," Tracy sniped, playfully frowning at me. "But he talking the right numbers and of course Reese already gave him the stamp of approval, so I say let's do this."

"So when you trying to get started?" Lance jumped in and asked.

"Based on the prices you all gave me, I'm ready to make my first order today," Bink let it be known.

"Well we don't keep no product at this warehouse, but we can make the trade tomorrow. Lance you go with Reese tomorrow to make the drop," I said feeling decent about the situation, but wanting to have someone keep a watchful eye until I felt good. Everybody in the crew had their strengths and one that Lance had was he analyzed everything. To the point that most of the time he overanalyzed. But he was sharp and it paid off for us on numerous occasions.

"That works for me. I'll see the two of you tomorrow," Bink said, nodding his head at Reese and Lance. "Nico, it was a pleasure. Let this be the beginning of a long and profitable business relationship."

"Yes, indeed," I said shaking his hand.

"I'll walk him out," Reese said following behind Bink.

"That money don't stop," Ritchie said once Reese and Bink had left the building.

"Pretty soon won't nobody be able to move drugs in New York without coming through us," Alton added.

"Boss, you awfully quiet. You got something on yo' mind," Lance questioned.

"I'm straight. Dude want a lot of product, but if he got the money to pay then he can play. We'll see," I said not yet convinced how legitimate Bink was.

"I think nigga legit," Ritchie said.

"Me too," Alton cosigned.

"Hell he better be! Don't nobody got time for a motherfucker to be playing," Tracy popped.

"Exactly, but enough of this shit. I got some other things to handle. Everything straight with business?" I asked before I headed out.

"I already checked in with all our workers and shit is running smoothly. I'll do another check in a few hours," Ritchie informed me.

"Cool. Running smoothly is always music to my ears," I said.

"Well, I'm right behind you, Nico. I'm picking my girl Angie up from work today so we can go have some drinks."

"Angela. I actually ran into her this morning."

"Where the hell did you run into Angie at?"

"At the deli around the corner from her job."

"Oh really?! Ain't that some shit. What the hell did you all talk about?"

"Calm down pitbull, you letting that green eye monster show." Alton laughed.

"Oh shut the hell up, Alton. Mind yo' business. This between me and Nico," Tracy snapped. "So tell me, Nico what did you all talk about?" Tracy continued, not letting up.

"I got her number and I plan on taking her out on a date."

"So you know, it won't no damn coincidence that Angie ran into you. I told her you be going to that deli."

"I know she told me."

"I should've known, Angie can't hold water. Nico, don't mess with that girl. I know she might appear like she about that life, but she ain't."

"Tracy, what you mean by that?"

"You know what the fuck I mean, Nico. Angie is my girl and I know you think because we're friends she must be hip, but she ain't."

"Tracy, it's a date. Calm down." I chuckled. "You getting all worked up over nothing."

"Okay, you say that now... that damn Angie, she just had to track you down," Tracy said shaking her head. "Let me get outta here."

"Don't go messing shit up for me neither and scare that girl off. I promise I'ma treat her right," I said putting my arms up. Tracy simply gave me the nigga face and left.

"Man, you know that girl like you. I don't know why you be playin' wit' her." Alton laughed, then slapped hands with Ritchie.

"We all know the rules including Tracy. No dating amongst the crew," I said without hesitation.

"That don't stop her from liking you though," Ritchie said.

"I like Tracy too but rules are rules. She's more like a sister to me anyway. A fine ass sister, but still a sister. Now Angie on the other hand, is fine too and she's not off limits. Tracy will be a'ight, trust me. Now enough fuckin' around wit' you knuckleheads, let me go." I swung my hand, dismissing them in a joking way.

On the way to my car I noticed Reese, Bink, and Tracy talking outside. They waved in my direction and I put my hand up saluting them. Bink seemed to be fitting right in nicely making me slightly optimistic that this might be the beginning of a profitable business relationship.

Chapter 13

Don't Be Afraid

"First you call, now we're here having dinner. All within two days, although it took three weeks to make it happen," Angela commented as she took another sip of her wine.

"I apologize for that. Business got crazy. I had to go out of town a few times and every time I was about to call you I got sidetracked. But I'm glad you still picked up once I finally did."

"Can't lie, I was reluctant, but how could I re-sist dinner at some super fancy restaurant in the city. First you bring flowers now this place. You re-ally do know how to show a girl a good time."

"You deserve more, but I didn't want to over do it. You know, come on too strong."

"From what I heard, going strong is what Nico Carter does best."

"Is that right? Let me guess, you heard that from Tracy."

"Tracy only speaks highly of you. Between you and me, I think Tracy has a crush on you, but she would never admit it. But I guess it would be hard for any woman not to."

"I don't know about that, Angela. I know you said everybody calls you Angie, but you look like an Angela to me. Do you mind that?"

"Of course not, it's my name and I like the way you say it anyway." Angela blushed.

"There you go blushing again."

"For some reason every time I'm around you, I find myself blushing."

"Why is that?"

"Maybe because you have looks, money, charm, and if what the streets say are true, a lot of power. That can be very alluring and also very scary."

"Don't be afraid, Angela," I said, putting my hand across the table to touch hers. There were candles placed on each table and the way the light hit her face, she seemed to be glowing. Her pink lipgloss made her plump full lips even more inviting. Her short, jet-black tapered haircut accentuated her high cheekbones and the fitted black dress she was wearing accentuated Angela's other assets too.

"This is going to sound crazy, but I know I should be afraid of you. I know you're probably going to break my heart, but I don't care. I've played it safe all my life, but I don't want to do that with you."

"Then don't. I'm young, I'm making moves and I'm not really in the position to be in a serious relationship. But I can promise that I'll always try to show you a good time. There's something about you that I like, Angela and I want the chance for us to get to know each other better."

"I want that, too. I won't put any pressure on you. I'll follow your lead and whatever happens… happens."

"If you keep that attitude we might go far." I winked before calling the waiter over so we could place our dinner order. I made that statement to Angela in a joking way, but I was being serious on the low. Angela's laid back calm demeanor fit how I was living right now perfectly. She seemed headache free and that was the number one criteria for any woman to be in my life. Most women didn't even make it to a first date with me. After a couple of phone conversations they were quickly deleted off the list because it was obvious to me that emotionally they were too high maintenance. Angela seemed different which was what I needed because street niggas need love too.

"So we low on product already?" I huffed as Lance and I stood by our cars talking in front of Fulton Park.

"I know, but since Bink became a customer he be re-upping damn near every week which seems to now be interfering with our other clients. We need more product man. That ain't a bad thing."

"It is if you can't get it. I think I'm maxing out my connect. It might be time for me to get another." I sighed.

"You been dealing wit' yo' guy since Uncle Marvin and he was your uncle's connect. You really want to replace him?"

"I didn't say nothing about replacing him just having a back up. Business is growing. We have to keep up or risk leaving the door cracked for some-one else to come in and take some of our business. I just want to be proactive," I explained.

"That makes sense. Do you have somebody in mind?"

"A couple people. But this dude Fernando that I've done some business with told me about this one connect that seems promising. I have to see who has the better product, best prices, and how quickly they can deliver though. Finding a new con-nect is now at the top of my priority list. Until then slow down how much product you give Bink. I have to make sure our other clients get served too."

"I'll handle it," Lance said tossing the soda he was drinking in the trashcan. "It won't be a problem."

"It's only temporary, at least that's what I'm hoping. Regardless, we'll make it work. But let me get outta here, I'm taking Angela to lunch."

"Angela... I've heard you mention her name quite a few times lately. What's up with that?"

"She's cool, I like her. I took her out to dinner for the first time a few weeks ago and we've been kickin' it ever since."

"This is a first for you. I ain't never known you to make time for no female and we been friends for years. All you think about is makin' money."

"And that ain't changed. I said I liked her. I ain't said we gettin' married. She a sweet girl and I can't lie, I enjoy her company. She don't give me no headaches either and it don't hurt that she easy on the eyes."

"You crazy." Lance laughed. "Hell, I'm just glad to know you still interested in women. I was gettin' worried," Lance cracked.

"Nigga, get off my dick. Don't worry 'bout my female situation. I'm straight over here. Don't be mad at me 'cause yo' ass been on lockdown wit' the same chick since high school," I joked.

"Fuck you! I thought you liked Morgan."

"Man, I do. I was jokin' wit' yo' sensitive ass. Morgan's a good girl. She gotta be to put up wit' yo' anal ass. Trust me, ain't that many good girls left so stick with what you got," I advised Lance. I meant that shit too. The line of business we were in, you rarely ran across a decent chick, especially one you could trust. Lance lucked out by still being with Morgan after all these years and I hoped he appreciated what he had. If not, I def wanted to remind him.

"I know I got a good woman. I didn't wanna say nothing 'cause she won't know for sure until she goes to the doctor tomorrow, but Morgan thinks she's pregnant," Lance revealed with the biggest smile on his face that I had ever seen.

"Word! Nigga, you gon' be a daddy!"

"I think so, at least I hope so. I've been wantin' a seed for a minute now, but Morgan insisted we wait until she finished college. Then she got a job and wanted to wait some more. I guess all that love-making I put on her finally paid off," Lance bragged.

"Shut yo' corny ass up," I clowned. "But on the real if Morgan is pregnant, congratulations. You gon' be a hell of a father. You a good dude," I said patting Lance's shoulder.

"Thank you. I appreciate that, especially coming from you. Does that mean you'll be the Godfather? I mean you do got all the money." Lance laughed. "So what you say." Lance continued laughing, rubbing his hands together. "But seriously, if Morgan and I are blessed with a baby, there is nobody else I would want to be the Godfather but you."

"I wouldn't have it no other way. We family, I got nothing but love for you. Now let me get the hell out of here," I said looking down at my watch.

"You 'bout to make me late for my lunch date with Angela."

"The way things are going with Angela, a lil' Nico might be next."

"Save your jokes. It'll be a long time before we see a lil' Nico," I said and drove off.

Chapter 14

Connect

"I'll be out of town for five days. While I'm gone, I need for ya to stay on top of shit. As we all know product is low so we have to move what we got with caution," I informed my crew as I sat at the round table with Lance, Ritchie, Alton, Reese, and Tracy.

"We gettin' a lot of complaints in the streets. They saying we dried up. How long you think this drought gon' last?" Ritchie questioned.

"That's the reason I'm going to the Dominican Republic, to fix this shit."

"Are you sure you'll be able to?" Reese then asked.

"I won't be sure of nothing until I get that

motherfuckin' product in my hand. But I am optimistic. If I wasn't I wouldn't be making this trip."

"Nico, I learned a long time ago not to ever doubt you 'cause you always come through. This ain't nothing but a slight bump in the road. I know you got this," Alton said pumping up his fist.

"I'll be in touch with Lance on a daily basis checking in, but of course get at me," I said, making eye contact with each of them, "if anything comes up. Other than that, we done here. I'll see you when I get back."

As we all got up from the table, Tracy strutted her ass in my direction. She was mad quiet during our meeting and I had a pretty good idea why.

"So you taking Angie with you to the Dominican Republic?" Tracy said in an accusatory type way.

"Tracy, you obviously already know the answer to that question so why are you even asking me?"

"Why are you doing this, Nico?"

"Doing what... living my life?"

"No, playing with Angie's."

"Tracy, you know I love you, we family, but don't nobody question me about my personal life. I don't owe you or anybody else an explanation. I'ma need you to slow down, 'cause you pushing it and it's rubbing me the wrong way."

"Sorry to be rubbing you the wrong way, Nico, but I have every right to be concerned about my girl."

"Concerned? She's a grown fuckin' woman. What's the real issue, Tracy?"

"I told you what my issue is. Oh I get it... you think I'm jealous of your relationship with Angie."

"I don't know what to think... are you jealous?" I straight up asked.

"No, that's some bullshit. Angie's mother used to babysit me. Angie was a few years younger than me, but we became really close. I was like a big sister to her. When she was 14, Angie's mother died, but while she was sick she made me promise to watch over her daughter and not let anything happen to her. Like you, Nico, I try to keep my promises. I'm a woman of my word."

"I get that and I respect it, but you know me. I have no intentions of hurting Angela so stop worrying. Your girl is good in my hands... I promise."

"I'ma hold you to that, Nico, but my gut is telling me, this shit ain't gon' end well. Have a good trip," Tracy said sarcastically before grabbing her purse and leaving.

I stood there shaking my head for a few seconds. I now had a better understanding of why Tracy was so protective of Angela, but I still felt she was out of pocket. I felt she was overreacting and coming at me like I was some type of bad guy. But I had to accept the fact that only time would ease Tracy's mind. Tracy was fair and once she realized that I wasn't going to bring Angela any harm, her attitude would change.

When we arrived at the resort in Punta Cana, the first thing Angela wanted to do was chill on the beach until we arrived at the private luxury home located in a gated community. This was the first time I had ever been to the Dominican Republic, but the potential connect I was meeting with suggested this is where I should stay and I'm glad I listened. I had never seen such beauty in person before. Growing up in the grimy streets of Brooklyn, I almost forgot places like this existed.

After handling my business, I planned on spending the duration of the trip with Angela racing on speedboats, deep-sea sport fishing, snorkeling, whale watching, catamaran sailing, and even swimming with dolphins. On our final night there, I was going to surprise her with a candlelight dinner on a small island called Catalina. I had everything figured out and I was looking forward to making this a trip Angela would never forget.

"Did I die and go to heaven because this can't be real." Angela gasped when she stepped out on the humongous balcony that overlooked a golf course, private pool, gazebo, and white sandy beaches with the bluest water I had ever seen.

"If this is what heaven looks like, I see why everybody tryna get there. You still want to hit the beach or do you wanna take a dip in that pool?" I said, hugging Angela from behind.

"I think I'll pass on the beach and dive into that pool instead," Angela replied, turning her head to kiss me.

"Then I guess you better go put on that bikini," I said kissing her back.

"Who needs a bathing suit." Angela giggled slipping out of her halter dress and panties right there before heading towards the pool. "Are you just going to stand there or are you coming?" Angela giggled some more, running towards the pool.

The way the hot sun was hitting her golden brown skin had a nigga feeling some type of way. Her body was glistening and I couldn't do nothing, but watch as Angela's curvy body dived in the water. After soaking in how damn sexy she was, I stepped out of my linen shorts and shirt and joined her.

"Did I tell you how amazing you are," were the first words out of Angela's mouth when she rose from the water to catch her breath.

"Nah, you haven't," I said pulling her body close to me.

"You are. You didn't have to bring me to this amazing place, but you did. This is the nicest thing anyone has ever done for me."

"This is only the beginning. I have big plans for you."

"That's funny because I have plans for you too," Angela teased biting down on my bottom lip.

That night Angela showed me exactly what her plans were. She gave me the best head of my life. I don't know if being in a fucking five bedroom beachfront palace heightened the sexiness, but Angela's lips wrapped around my rock hard dick felt even better than usual. She must've felt the same way because her moans of pleasure were on fever pitch when I slid inside. Her pussy was even wetter than the pool we had just finished swimming in. After that night, there was no doubt in my mind that Angela was a keeper.

The next day on my way to meet with my potential connect, Marco, I placed a call to Lance to see how shit was going. "What up my dude... how's it going?"

"Everything is cool under the circumstances. How did things go on your end?"

"I'm on my way to meet with Marco now. I'll hit you up as soon as I'm done," I said trying to pay attention to where I was going while talking to Lance.

"Cool. I'm keeping my fingers crossed this shit works out 'cause man we need it, we need it bad," Lance said sounding somewhat antsy.

"You sure everything a'ight over there. I ain't

been gone, but for a day and you sounding mad shaky."

"I'm straight just looking into a few things."

"Looking into what? Is there something going on that I need to know about?"

"Not right now. You know I'll let you know if that changes."

"You better."

"Nico, you already know how we do. I'm not gonna keep you in the dark about shit. It's probably nothing, but if I'm wrong you'll be the second to know."

"Okay. I'm here so I gotta go, but I'ma call you when I'm done."

"I'll be waiting on that call," Lance said and then hung up. He left me with a funny feeling when we got off the phone. I didn't know what was going on with Lance, but he didn't sound like himself. I couldn't worry about that right now though because I had to handle this meeting. But finding out what had Lance sounding shaky was next on my agenda.

"You finally made it," Marco said greeting me at the door, which surprised me. For some reason I thought bodyguards would surround him and he would have an entourage, but it wasn't the type of party. Marco was on some real chill shit. He lived in what I would consider a modest house on the beach, especially since he was supposed to be one of the largest coke and heroin distributors in the

Dominican Republic. He was also much older than I expected.

"I appreciate you seeing me, Marco," I said taking a seat in the living room area. The doors were wide open and the breeze from the beach was blowing the cream sheer silk curtains. The vibe was so tranquil that I almost forgot what the fuck I was there for. Now I understood why Marco lived here. There was something about the place that completely put your mind at ease.

"Of course. Fernando speaks very highly of you. He says you are in a bit of a bind, I believe I can help," Marco said speaking in broken English.

"That's what I needed to hear," I said, welcoming the good news. If Marco could be my new connect and I could get the product at the prices I wanted, I would be much closer to building my multi-million dollar drug empire.

Chapter 15

Guilt Trip

"Man, I'm happy you back," Lance said when we met up at a bar over in Queens. It was a low-key spot we would go to periodically to discuss business over drinks.

"It's good to be back."

"If it was me... the beaches, the sun... I would've stayed my ass over there."

"A little relaxation is nice once in awhile, but my high comes from these streets. Although it was a business trip mixed wit' pleasure, I won't need to take a vacation for at least another two or three years."

"Man you ain't right, but your way of thinking makes you the great Nico Carter. So let's get down

to what you really came to discuss... business."
Lance smiled.

"Before we get to that, how's Morgan doing?"

"She driving me crazy, but her pregnancy is
going great."

"Ain't that what pregnant women supposed to
do... drive you crazy." We laughed. "But good, you
know I gotta check on my future Godchild. You let
me know if you guys need anything. Now that we
got that out the way, let's discuss business," I said,
signaling my hand for another round of drinks.

"Shit is looking good now that you came
through with this new connect. Do you have any
idea when the first shipment will arrive?"

"No later than Friday, Marco said."

"Well, motherfuckers just gon' have to wait. I
mean ain't nothing we can do."

"How bad is it? We don't have enough to maintain until Friday? I told you to spread that shit out.
We can't be completely wiped out."

"There was a slight problem, nothing major."

"Is that why you were sounding all shaky when
I spoke to you in the Dominican Republic? When I
called you back you said everything had been handled and shit was straight. Was that a lie?" I grilled
Lance.

"No, it wasn't a lie. At first I thought there was
a problem, but then Reese told me everything was
good, but then..." Lance hesitated.

"But then what?"

"But then Reese told me that he fulfilled Bink's order not realizing that was the last bit of product we had. It was a miscommunication."

"So wait, we runnin' 'round here dry while Bink got all the product? What type of shit does that make? We supposed to be the distributor not the other fuckin' way around."

"Nico, I know. It was an honest mistake. But luckily things came through with Marco and we'll have plenty of product to fulfill orders no later than Friday. Nobody got our quality of product and prices so our customers will wait."

"That ain't the point, Lance. Ya can't be making mistakes like that. We running a drug operation, but ain't got no drugs. I specifically said to slow down how much product we give Bink until I got this situation under control. Yet that nigga end up wit' the last bit of what we got. Don't neva let no dumb shit like that happen again."

"It won't."

"It bet not. I count on you to stay on top of shit, Lance. This some knucklehead shit I would expect from Alton, or maybe Ritchie 'cause he caught up in some pussy, but not you." I huffed.

"I know. I thought I had told Reese that was all we had left and we couldn't sell to Bink, but I fucked up. I guess my mind has been on the baby and Morgan's pregnancy. I apologize, Nico, but I'm back focused, man."

"I understand. Luckily more product is on the

way, but just know you've used your one free pass. Now let me finish this drink," I said, needing something to take the edge off.

"I can't believe how good you treat me." Angela grinned as I paid for the clothes I just bought her. We left with so many bags you would've thought we shut down the store.

"I like treating you good," I said holding the door open for her.

"I like you treating me good, too. I can't wait to wear that red dress tonight when we go to Tracy's birthday party.

"I can't wait to take it off of you," I said about to open the passenger car door for Angela.

"Babe, wait," Angela said looking down. "What's wrong?"

"I left one of the bags in the store."

"You sure?"

"Positive. I don't see the bag that had two pairs of shoes in it."

"You get in the car, I'll go back inside and get the bag," I said heading back towards the store. Those were the last words I said before everything seemed to move in slow motion. Out of nowhere, a car pulled up next to mine with a guy wearing a black ski mask. His eyes locked with mine before he stuck his head out and began blasting. It all happened so fast that I didn't even have an opportunity to reach in the car to retrieve my gun.

"Angela, get down!" I yelled out, leaping towards her. All I heard was glass shattering. Then I saw bags and clothes flying everywhere. As quickly as the gunshots rang out they instantly came to a halt. When I reached Angela all the clothes concealed her. In rapid speed I began tossing the clothes off of her and underneath there was Angela's dead body covered in blood.

By the time I finished getting interviewed by the cops, it was nighttime and I was in a daze. Just a few hours earlier, Angela was shopping, smiling, and giving me her signature giggle and now she was dead. I had killed before, had seen people get killed, but holding Angela's dead body in my arms fucked with me in a way that I had never experienced.

"Where's Tracy?" I asked Alton when I got to the lounge where Tracy was having her birthday party.

"Damn, it's good to see you too, Nico, what happened to hello?" Alton joked.

"Not right now, Alton. I'm not in the mood," I said, dreading the conversation I was about to have with Tracy.

"Is everything okay?" Alton asked with concern.

"No, now where is Tracy?"

"She's over in the back. Listen, I..." Before Alton could even finish his sentence I was headed to the back to find Tracy. She was sitting with two of her girlfriends drinking champagne when I walked up.

"Hey, Nico! Where's my girl Angie?" she beamed, standing up and coming in my direction. "And where is my present? I know you didn't show up to my birthday party empty handed," Tracy continued, sipping on her glass of champagne.

"We need to talk... in private." I sighed.

"Awww damn! You and Angie got into an argument and now she not coming to my party? Fuck that! I'm calling her right now," Tracy said, reaching into her purse to retrieve her cell phone.

"You can't call her, Tracy," I said, putting my hand over her purse.

"Why the fuck not? What is going on, Nico and why you actin' so fuckin' strange?"

"Can we just go talk in private," I said, leading Tracy by the arm towards a hallway I noticed. It led to some bathrooms and I pulled Tracy into one of them.

"Yo, what the fuck is going on?" Tracy snapped.

"There's no easy way to tell you this."

"Tell me what, Nico?"

"Angela is dead." The shock of hearing what I said caused Tracy to drop her glass and she stood in front of me with her mouth open, but no words were coming out. "It happened a few hours ago. We had just left the store and then there was a drive-by-shooting."

"A drive by! Damn, ya got caught up in somebody else's bullshit. Who was they shooting at?"

"Me."

"Wait, somebody was shooting at you and Angie got killed?" Tracy questioned as her bottom lip shivered.

"Yes. I'm sorry, Tracy. I know how much you cared about Angela and so did I," I said putting my hand on her shoulder.

"Don't touch me!" she yelled, jerking her body away from me. I told you this wasn't gon' end well. We live such a fucked up life, but we signed up for this shit, Angie didn't. I knew..." Tracy pointed her finger at my chest and paused for a second as she tried to hold back tears from flowing. "I knew no good would come from this relationship."

"Don't you think I feel fucked up about what happened too. I saw her die. I held her dead body in my arms. The guilt is eatin' my ass up inside. Yeah she died because of me, but I didn't pull the trigger."

"The moment you started dating Angie, you pulled the trigger. This is the shit I was talkin' 'bout, Nico. You the main one always stressing to us that this business ain't set up for love and relationships, but yet you had to get involved with someone who was like family to me, my own sister. I guess you understand why I practically begged you to let it go and not get involved with her. Now it's too late. My birthdays will never be the same again. Thanks for ruining it," Tracy stated, walking out the bathroom and leaving me standing in my own misery.

When I looked up I could see my reflection in the mirror. For the first time I didn't like what was staring back at me. No, I wasn't the ski-masked shooter, but Tracy was right, in a lot of ways I was the one that pulled the trigger.

Chapter 16

War Ready

"Any leads on who shot at me and killed Angela?" I asked Lance when he stopped by an office I had in downtown Brooklyn.

"Not yet," Lance admitted, taking a seat in the chair in front of my desk. He put his head down into his hands as completely stressed the fuck out.

"Has something else happened? 'Cause you seem out of your element."

"One of our trap houses got hit up late last night. I just found out about it on my way over here to see you."

"What the fuck!" I barked, pounding my fist down on the desk. "Which stash house?"

"Brownsville."

"How much product was there?"

"A lot. The shipment from Marco came in a couple of days ago and a big portion was at the Brownsville spot because we were expecting three big pickups today. It gets worse. They killed four of our workers that were there," Lance revealed.

"You can't be serious," I said standing in front of the window and staring outside. The sun was shining, but shit over my head was fuckin' gloomy.

"I don't think what happened is a coincidence or random. I think the same people that tried to kill you, hit up the stash house."

"No shit, Sherlock. Of course it ain't no fuckin' coincidence. It's the same motherfuckers. So you know what this means."

"What?" Lance said, looking up at me.

"It's means we 'bout to go to war."

"So you think it's a crew behind this?"

"Fuck yeah! Ain't one or two motherfuckers got enough balls to come at me like this. They tryna take me down and only a crew would think they have enough manpower to do so."

"So, what do you want to do?"

"First, we have to call a meeting and let everybody know what's going on because we all have to be on alert. They might've come at me first, but you, Tracy, Alton, Reese, and Ritchie could be next. We have to up security. Keep extra men posted outside each of the stash houses."

"I'll get on top of that immediately, but it's

gonna be hard to fight a war when we don't know who the enemy is," Lance said.

"You right. But let me handle that."

"Got you."

"In the meantime, let's get everybody war ready."

"It was a pleasant surprise to hear from you." I heard a familiar voice say behind me.

"My man, Bennie. I see you still like sneaking up on motherfuckers." I chuckled, shaking Bennie's hand. "Have a seat," I said, moving over so Bennie could sit next to me on the park bench.

"I haven't seen you since your Uncle Marvin passed away. You was just a boy, now you a man. Look at you." Bennie grinned. "You clean and handsome just like yo' daddy was. Yo' father sure was a good man," Bennie continued.

"He sure was."

"But I know you didn't call me to talk about yo' old man, may he rest in peace. They never did find the piece of shit responsible for killing him. That's a damn shame," Bennie said, shaking his head.

"Trust me, Bennie. I'm sure karma has found them and justice was served."

"I hope you right 'cause your father was a hell

of a man. But enough talkin' 'bout that, what can I do for you, Nico?"

"I need to utilize some of your street informants, that is if you're still in the business of handling that?"

"I am. Although I considered retiring that part of my business, after I couldn't find out any information about who killed your father. That shit ate me up for years." Bennie groaned.

"Don't be so hard on yourself. Things have a way of working themselves out. But I do hope you'll have better luck with me."

"Tell me what's going on?"

"A few weeks ago someone tried to kill me. They end up killing a young lady I was dating instead."

"Sorry to hear that."

"Yeah, she was a good girl who most def didn't deserve to die."

"So you looking to know who killed her so you can get that situation handled?"

"Yes, but I think it's a little deeper then one shooter. The other day one of my stash houses was hit and four of my men were killed. I think a competitor crew is tryna take me out. But I can't figure out who would even have the audacity to come at me."

"This new young cats out here so crazy. I don't know what they be thinking. Hell, they don't be thinking, but I believe I can help. I got some new kids working for me that I know if they had been around when your daddy had gotten killed, they would've got the motherfucker. They sharp and got their ears in everythang."

"Good. That's what I need. The sooner you can find out the better. My business is under attack. This shit ain't just taken money, it's taken lives. I don't want nobody else to die except for the people responsible for this mayhem."

"I'm about to put my people on it right now. Do you have any enemies you can think of?"

"None that I think is capable of pulling something like this off. But I could be wrong so don't sleep on nobody. Have your people check into everybody. Somebody knows what the fuck is going on who's behind it. So find out for me, Bennie."

"I got you, Nico. Your father came through for me on numerous occasions, so I owe it to him to help out his son."

"I appreciate that but best believe you come through for me you will be very well compensated."

"Thank you and I'll be in touch," Bennie said, shaking my hand before leaving.

After meeting with Bennie, I headed to the warehouse to meet up with my crew. When I pulled up, I saw that all their cars were parked out front so the only person they were waiting on was me.

"What's up fam," I said when I walked inside. They were immersed in a deep conversation so at first they didn't hear me. It took them a second to notice I had even come in.

"Nico, I'm glad you here," Alton said being the first person to spot me. "They over here arguing wit' each other," he explained.

"Listen, this ain't the time to be arguing amongst each other. What the fuck is you bickering about?" I barked, already annoyed before the meeting even started.

"Lance over here tryna dictate shit, when it's his fault four of our workers are dead," Ritchie spat.

"How the fuck is it my fault?" Lance shot back.

"You should've never had all that product in Brownsville. That ain't even our main spot. Normally only one at the most two men are posted there, but because you insisted on having all that product brought there we put more men on it. Now we lost money, our men, and drugs."

"Reese told me that we had three buyers coming through the next day to pick up their product," Lance explained.

"But I didn't say for you to have all their drugs there," Reese countered.

"It only made fuckin' sense to do it that way. The three buyers were closer to the Brownsville location," Lance said defending his decision.

"You mean it made sense to you," Ritchie grumbled.

"What the fuck would you have done, Ritchie? Oh I forgot, you be too busy running up in pussy to make a business decision," Lance quipped.

"Nigga, fuck you! My dick ain't got shit to do wit' the dumbass decision you made." Ritchie frowned.

"Everybody shut the fuck up!" I finally said. "You all are arguing over irrelevant shit. Whether or not Lance made the right decision having all that product at the Brownsville location don't change the fact that somebody tried to kill me and robbed one of the stash spots. We need to be spending our energy on tryna figure who the fuck is behind that shit instead of blaming each other. This shit is counterproductive. So have we amped up security?" I wanted to start discussing the important shit instead of the things we could no longer do anything about.

"Yes, I rallied a bunch of our men up and got them doubled up on the outside and inside for all locations. I even tripled them up on some of our busier spots," Reese said.

"That's good, Reese. I'm assuming you made sure everyone is properly armed?"

"No doubt. I even made sure they had plenty of backup on deck. Whoever these motherfuckers are that's coming for us, they'll be in for a rude awakening when they show up," Reese said confidently.

"I want each of you to have extra security on you too," I said.

"I don't need no extra security. I wish a moth-erfucker would step to me, they'll regret the day," Tracy popped, after being quiet for the entire time.

"That wasn't a suggestion, it's mandatory."

"What do you mean 'it's mandatory'?"

"We all know what the word mandatory means, including you, Tracy. So like I said, each of you have extra security at all time until this situa-tion is resolved," I made clear. I caught Tracy rolling her eyes, but I didn't care because being cautious was more important. I didn't want any more lives lost.

Chapter 17

Climax

It had been two weeks since the hit in Brownsville and we were no closer to finding out who was responsible. The only bright side was there hadn't been any new attacks, but in my gut, I had a bad feeling that something was about to go down. I didn't know why and the shit was fucking with me. As I sat alone in a booth at the bar in Queens, I felt I was about to go out of my mind trying to figure this thing out. So much wasn't adding up to me, like I was missing something, but I couldn't put my finger on it. I kept the drinks flowing determined to come up with something.

"Let me get what he's having."

"Tracy, what are you doing here?" I looked up

and said when I heard her talking to the waitress. "And where is your security?'

"Where is yours?" she asked right back.

"Nobody knows about this spot."

"Exactly. I thought it was the perfect opportunity to shake them motherfuckers and have some alone time. So, can I join you?"

"Be my guest. How did you know I was here?"

"Lance told me."

"I guess he didn't mention that I don't want to be bothered," I said knocking back another shot.

"He did, but I was hoping you would make an exception for me."

"Tracy, if you came here to talk more shit to me about Angela you can go 'head and leave now, 'cause I ain't here for it."

"I know I've been hard on you these last few months and I wanted to apologize."

"Apologize? Hmm, why apologize when you meant every word you said?"

"It's true I didn't want you to get involved with Angie, but it's not your fault that she's dead and I'm sorry for even putting that out there. I was hurt and angry, but I shouldn't have lashed out at you."

"I appreciate you saying that, but if Angela hadn't gotten involved with me, she would still be alive, living her life."

"Nico, Angela was well aware of the lifestyle you were living and she chose to get involved with you. I mean she was the one that came after you..."

remember. I remind myself of that every time I want to blame you for what happened to her."

"I guess..." I said as my voice trailed off.

"Don't do this to yourself, Nico. I know for a fact that Angela enjoyed every moment she spent with you. She said you made her feel more special than anyone has ever in her life."

"She said that?"

"Yes, she did. I have love for you anyway, but knowing that made me love you even more. You're one of the good guys, Nico. No matter how tough you try to act."

"One more, then I'm done," I said to the waitress when she stopped by the table to bring Tracy's drink. "How did shit get so bad so fast, Tracy? A couple months ago I felt we was unstoppable. Now..." I took a deep breath and shook my head.

"Now what?"

"Now I don't know what's gon' happen next."

"I know. We gonna find out who's behind all this bullshit and fuck them motherfuckers up. That's what's gon' happen next."

"Your feisty attitude is what I always loved most about you."

"And I thought it was the way I was able to handle a gun and look damn sexy doing it."

"That's a close second." I smiled. "But seriously, I hope you right, Tracy. "I'm ready for shit to get back to how it used to be."

"It will, Nico. Sooner than you think... watch.

We run these streets and whoever these dumb fucks are that decided to start a war with us, they will regret the day they made that decision."

"True dat," I said gulping down my last shot. "Now, let's go, 'cause if I have one more drink they'll have to drag me outta here."

"Don't let me find out you gettin' soft," Tracy joked, punching me in the arm.

"Never soft and you better take that back before I let this door hit you." I laughed, as I held the door open for Tracy.

"I ain't worried. All this ass I got will make that door bounce right back." She winked.

"Tracy, get down!" I yelled out.

"Huh!" she screamed, glancing back at me before looking in the direction I was staring at. Luckily, this time I was prepared and pulled out my gun shooting towards the man who was firing at us.

"Fuck you motherfucker!" Tracy bawled, pulling a gat from her purse and returning fire. At the exact same time both Tracy and me hit our mark. My bullet hit his chest and Tracy got the neck. After his body dropped, we didn't have a second to regroup when two more shooters popped out of nowhere with guns blazing.

"Tracy, you good?" I shouted to her as we both took cover behind a car.

"Of course I'm good. These niggas going down."

"You ready?" I said, motioning for us to come from behind the car and start blasting.

"Let's do this." Tracy nodded, as we began firing one shot after another. On the third try, Tracy put a bullet in the back of one of the shooters as he was turning away to take cover. I was able to shoot the other guy in his leg, which caused him to fall down in the middle of the street. I quickly ran towards him and put a bullet in his head to finish him off.

"Tracy, behind you! I yelled out when I noticed another gunman sneaking up on her. I fired off three more shots, but I wasn't fast enough. The gunman was able to release his shots, riddling Tracy's upper body with bullets before my shot blew his brains out.

"Nico," Tracy mumbled as blood flowed from her mouth.

"Shhh... shhh, don't say anything. Everything is gonna be fine. Tracy, I'ma get you some help," I reassured her.

"It's too late," she said softly. "We did good... if only that last motherfucker didn't show up," Tracy said, barely audible.

"Don't say another word. You have to keep your strength," I said, trying to stay strong.

"I love you, Nico, and make sure you get the motherfuckers who did this to me," Tracy said before closing her eyes.

"Tracy... Tracy... Tracy!" I kept yelling as I held her limp body. This was like reliving Angela's murder all over again only worse.

"This was a beautiful service, Nico," one of the guests at Tracy's funeral came over and said to me as I watched her coffin lowered in the ground.

"Thank you," I said not looking up. Even with the dark tinted sunglasses I was wearing, I felt it couldn't conceal the pain I was in. I must've been standing there forever because by the time I looked up, the only people left there was my security, Lance, Reese, Alton, and Ritchie.

"We need to get going, Nico," Lance said, putting his hand on my shoulder.

"Just give me a few more minutes." I needed a little bit more time to say goodbye to Tracy. Out of all the people to die, I didn't understand why it had to be her. First Angela and now Tracy, it was all too much. For the first time since I stepped into the drug game, I was asking myself was it really worth it? Was the high I got from hustling worth the lives of people I loved?

"What's next, boss?" Alton questioned as we all rode in the limo, headed towards a restaurant where a gathering was being held in Tracy's honor. I wasn't in the mood to attend, but I knew it was expected of me to show up. I'm sure Tracy would've wanted a party, but her family, specifically her mother, wanted a luncheon so I obliged. None of it mattered though because it wouldn't bring Tracy back.

"We've already beefed up security, all we can do is keep our ears to the streets and pray that we're prepared for whatever comes next," I said, staring out the window.

"Man, these pieces of shit are gonna burn for what they did to Tracy," Reese said bawling his fist.

"We have to find them first. These niggas startin' to feel like ghosts." Ritchie grumbled.

"I know right," Lance said, leaning down on his hand as if in deep thought. While they continued talking amongst each other, a text came through on my phone from Bennie asking me to call him. I didn't want to talk to him in front of my crew since no one was aware that I had hired Bennie.

"I'll be in there shortly," I told everyone when we arrived to the restaurant. Once they were all out of the limo and I was alone, I immediately called Bennie.

"I was beginning to worry when it took so long for you to call me," was the first thing Bennie said when he answered his phone.

"I was around some people and couldn't talk. I hope this call isn't a waste of my time."

"Not at all. I have some information that you definitely want to hear, but I prefer to tell you in person," Bennie said.

"I prefer that, too. I have to go inside to this restaurant for a second and then I'm coming straight to you."

"Meet at the regular spot?"

"Yep, I'll see you in about an hour," I said, ending the call. I planned on spending no more than 15 minutes inside the restaurant because the only thing on my mind, was finding out what Bennie had to say.

Chapter 18

Broken

"Bennie, I apologize for being late, but I got tied up," I said when I sat down next to him on the park bench.

"No problem, I know you a busy man, Nico."

"That had nothing to do with it. Today was a member of my crew's funeral. Her name was Tracy. She was family to me and now she's gone. That's why I hope you have something for me because this is hitting way too close to home now."

"I do. I know exactly who is trying to bring you and your crew down. His name is Bink."

"The nigga that buys product from me... that Bink?"

"That's the one. A few weeks ago you went

through a time when you ran out of product, correct?"

"Yeah, how did you know that?"

"Well, that Bink fella used that to his advantage and was supplying to some of your clientele during your drought. He used a middleman of course so you wouldn't know it was coming from him."

"So Bink was buying up all my product so he could then sell to my clients. That sonofabitch."

"From what my street informant found out, you were able to get a new connect."

"True."

"Once Bink knew you would have enough product to supply your customers, he decided it was time to take you out," Bennie explained.

"That motherfucker," I said, feeling my blood boil. "But something ain't adding up," I said, looking over at Bennie.

"There's more. This is the final piece to the puzzle," Bennie said, leaning forward.

"I'm listening."

On my way to the warehouse, I kept replaying every word Bennie said to me. I remembered each detail as if it had been engraved in my brain. I had already made the necessary calls to track Bink down and now I was on my way to meet with my crew. When I arrived at the warehouse, I damn near jumped out the car before my driver even had an opportunity to turn it off.

"I'm glad all of you are here," I said when I got inside.

"You said it was an emergency, so we all got here as soon as possible," Lance said.

"Yeah, what's going on? Don't tell me somebody else has been killed?" Ritchie asked nervously.

"No, not yet. But I know who's responsible for all the fucked up shit that's been going on."

"Get out! Who? Let's go kill them motherfuckers," Alton shouted. "I knew you'd find out who it was, Nico," Alton continued getting amped.

"Bink."

"Bink, as in the nigga that buy product from us?" Ritchie asked, looking shocked.

"Yeah, that Bink."

"Are you sure, Nico?" Reese questioned.

"I'm positive."

"Then we need to make our move... now!" Alton barked.

"I'm working on it, but I don't know his location. It's like he disappeared. When is the last time he made a buy?"

"A few days ago. So unless he got wind that you were on to him and decided to leave town, he has to still be around," Lance reasoned.

"I only found out today so Bink shouldn't know

anything is up. As far as he's concerned, shit is still sweet for him and I want to keep it that way until we locate him."

"That slick motherfucker. I can't believe this nigga was doing business wit' us and plotting on us at the same time. That bitch ass nigga going down," Alton sulked.

"Yeah, that nigga do got a lot of balls. I'm just glad you figured this shit out, Nico, so we can shut him down for good," Reese said. "So how do you want to move on this?"

"Since you and Lance are the ones he primarily deals with, hit him up and see if he can meet with you tonight. If he can't meet with you then at least try and get his whereabouts."

"Sure, you want me to call him now?" Reese asked.

"Yeah, call him now."

"It's ringing," Reese mouthed as he held the phone to his ear. "He ain't answering," he said.

"Hang up," I said.

"Do you want me to try and call him?" Lance suggested.

"No, that might raise suspicions with Reese calling first and then you calling right behind him."

"You want me to send him a text message telling him to call me back?" Reese asked.

"That's a good idea. Send the text and if he responds you know what to do," I said.

"I'm on it."

"Is there anything you want us to do?" Lance wanted to know.

"Not right now."

"At least we finally know who the enemy is. Only if we had found out sooner, Tracy would still be alive," Ritchie said sadly.

"I know. We weren't able to save Tracy, but we will make sure everybody responsible for her death pays with their life," I stated. "I wanted to keep everybody in the loop on what was going on. Now that I have, you all can go and we'll meet back up tomorrow."

"Nico, is there anything you need me to do?" Lance came over and asked me as everyone was heading out.

"Just be careful. We'll talk tomorrow," I said walking out with him.

"I will. I'll be home chillin' with Morgan, rubbing on her pregnant belly." Lance smiled. "But call me if anything comes up," Lance said before getting in his car.

"Take me to my office," I directed my driver. I then placed a phone call to see if the men I had hunting down Bink made any progress. "Any news?"

"Not yet, but we're on it," he assured me.

"Trust me, they'll be movement very soon... I promise you. I'll be expecting a call soon."

"Okay," the worker said not sounding as confident as me, but I wasn't worried.

I wasn't at my office for more than an hour

when my cell went off. As I expected, it was one of my workers calling me back. "You got a location?"

"Yep, just like you said we would."

"Good, text me the address. Don't let them leave. I'm on the way," I said, putting on my bullet-proof vest.

When I arrived at the address the worker gave me, I had my driver park next to the men I had keeping an eye on Bink. Luckily, it wasn't far so I was able to get there quickly. "How many inside?" I asked.

"We've counted four."

"Cool. I'm sure they're armed, but they won't be a match for us. How many men we got?"

"I already have seven surrounding the back of the apartment building and another seven parked up the street, waiting for the green light."

"Give them the green light then and let's go." With my two bodyguards we were over 15 men deep, about to ambush Bink and what made the shit so beautiful was he didn't even see it coming. "Kick that door down," I ordered, knowing the element of surprise would work in our favor.

"What the fuck!" Bink stood up and barked as his front door busted open. His immediate reaction was to reach for his firearm that was on the couch, but when he saw all the guns pointing at his head he knew better.

"Don't even think about it," I said to Bink who looked like he was about to shit on himself.

"I knew you would lead me to him, Reese. Thank you."

"Yo, Nico, I was just about to call you and let you know I found Bink. I'm glad you finally here," Reese said, standing up from the chair he was sitting in and coming towards me. I nodded my head to one of the gunmen and he immediately put the gun to Reese's head. "Why the fuck you got that gun pointed in my face?" Reese shrugged and then looked over at me as if he thought I would tell the gunmen to aim his weapon elsewhere.

"Killing you," I said pointing at Reese, "is what I'm most looking forward to."

"Nico, what the fuck is you talkin' about?" Reese was trying to give his best impression of a confused individual, but the shit wasn't working.

"The jig is up, so stop. I know it was you orchestrating all this bullshit wit' Bink. Nigga, you was part of a team and you killed one of the members. Tracy is dead because of yo' punk ass. I should shoot you right now, but that would be too easy. You will suffer... I promise. Your death will be long, painful, and slow."

"Nico, man this is all a misunderstanding. I can explain everything. If you hear me out it will all make sense... please," Reese begged.

"And Bink, for yo' fat ass to think you could take my spot. Oh wait, did dumb and dumber plan to share the position. You clowns disgust me. Tie all these niggas up, including these two motherfuckers sitting there not saying shit," I directed my men. I figured the two men were some workers of Bink, but I didn't give a fuck who they were because they were dying tonight too.

"Nico, it was all Reese's idea. He set this shit in motion from the jump. He brought me on. I wasn't even buying the drugs. He was stealing from you. It was him that wanted to takeover. When you found that new connect Reese decided it was time for you to go and make his move. It was all him... I swear."

"Bink, shut the fuck up! He's lyin', Nico!" Reese shouted sounding like the snake he was.

"None of this shit matters, both of you are gonna die."

"Man, I don't wanna die. It wasn't supposed to end like this," Bink said, sounding like he was about to break down in tears.

"Tie these niggas up," I said, ready to get this over with."

"Wait... wait... wait," Bink said nervously as one of the men was about to place tape over his mouth. "I know something. I'll tell you if you just let me live."

I saw Reese's face frown up and his jaw start flinching. "Nico, you don't need to listen or believe anything this nigga has to say. He making up bullshit to try and take the crew down. It's divide and conquer. I promise I'm not working wit' this nigga. He got a partner, but it ain't me," Reese said, pleading his case.

"All lies," I scuffed. "Tell me what you know, Bink, and I might consider letting you live."

"Once Reese realized my cover was blown, he said he needed to move quickly so he had me call some guys to take care of Ritchie and Lance," Bink revealed.

"Take care how?" I asked, but was afraid to hear the answer.

"Kill..."

Before Bink could even complete his thought, I was on the phone calling Lance. "Pick up the phone, Lance!" I called him again, and when he still didn't answer I called Ritchie.

"What up, man," Ritchie answered.

"Has anybody been to your crib?"

"I don't know, I'm not home. I'm at this chick's crib," Ritchie said.

"Have you heard from Lance?"

"No, not since we left the warehouse, why what's wrong?"

"Listen, get over to Lance's crib ASAP. Reese sent some men over there to kill him."

"What the fuck! Our nigga, Reese? Nah, man you must be mistaken," Ritchie said in denial.

"I'll explain the shit to you later. Right now you just get over to Lance's crib and bring some backup. I'll keep trying his cell, but call me as soon as you get to his place," I said, ready to break my phone out of anger, but instead used the butt of my gun to pistol whip Reese. Blood instantly gushed from the side of his head. I was tempted to finish him off right then, but that would be letting him off too easy.

"Get these motherfuckers and take them to the spot. When you get there, you can go 'head and kill Bink and these two other fucks, but don't kill Reese. Torture his ass, but leave him alive and lucid. I'll finish him off once I get there. I'ma stop by Lance's crib first. Call me if there's a problem, but don't fuck this shit up," I said rushing out.

On the way over to Lance's crib, I kept calling him, but wasn't getting an answer and now Ritchie wasn't answering his phone. After about 15 minute, we finally arrived to Lance's crib and when we turned onto the street there was an ambulance and several police cars out front.

"Stop the car!" I shouted, jumping out the back of the SVU and running over to the crowd of people.

"Nico, man I was just about to call you, but I was trying to find out what happened first," Ritchie said, stepping away from the large group of people standing around.

"What happened?"

"I'm not sure. All I know is there was a shooting and it came from Lance's brownstone. I haven't found out anything else yet," Ritchie explained.

Right after Ritchie spoke, I saw them bringing

out the first body on the stretcher. The body was covered up and I was praying that Lance managed to turn the table and kill the intruder. "Excuse me," I said walking away from Ritchie and over to a crime scene unit member who was carrying out the body on a gurney.

"Yes?"

"My brother lives there, can I please see if that's him?" He looked at me for a second then down at the body as if debating my request. "Please?" I guess he could hear the pleading in my voice because without saying a word he showed me the face. He quickly recovered it and proceeded out.

For a second I thought my knees were about to buckle as I felt my legs were locked and I couldn't move. Then I noticed them bringing out another body covered up and the large pregnant stomach was obvious. "Not Morgan and the baby too," I said as this sharp pain shot through my chest. "They got them... Lance and Morgan. Man, she was pregnant. How they kill that woman knowing she had a child growing inside of her," I said to Ritchie when he came over to me.

"And Reese is responsible for this bullshit! What the fuck! Damn," Ritchie said shaking his head in dismay. "What part of the game is this?"

I didn't even know how to respond to what Ritchie said because I didn't know what part of the game this was myself. We were a family, a crew. We came up together and built an empire and now the shit had completely crumbled. This part of the game had left me broken.

When I got to the spot we used to dispose of bodies before calling in the cleanup crew, Reese was sitting in a chair, bloody and battered, but very much alive. His eyes were halfway closed. Partly because they were bloody and busted and also it appeared he was falling asleep.

"Wake his ass up," I said to one of my workers. They splashed a bucket of water over his face, which shook him out of his slump.

"Man, can you go 'head and kill me so we can get this shit over wit'," Reese mumbled.

"If I had the time, I would keep you alive for the next 10 years and damn near kill you and bring you back to life to only damn near kill you again. Unfortunately, I have too much shit to take care and honestly, you ain't even worth the stress. I mean, you have to be the foulest type of nigga to have a pregnant woman killed."

"Fuck you, Nico! These streets got you thinking you Mr. Untouchable. Now you wanna act like you a saint. We supposed to be a crew, but we all gotta kiss yo' ass and bow down to you. I could've stepped in your shoes and ran this shit."

"Is that right? You would've run this shit with who? Your cousin Alton, is that who? Was he in on this with you too?"

"Hell no! His punk ass is another Nico Carter ass kisser. That nigga would've ran and told you everything."

"So why not kill him? I get why you tried to kill me. But you took out Tracy, then Lance, and you would've got Ritchie if he had been home so why not Alton?"

"'Cause he family. He work my nerve, but we do have the same blood and my mom would've killed me if she ever found out I had my own cousin murdered. 'Cause like I said, we are family."

"And to think I thought we were family, too," I said and just put one bullet between his eyes. Reese wasn't even worth more than that.

A few minutes later my men brought Alton in who seemed completely baffled. "Nico, what's going on? These guys just showed up at my crib and brought me here. Is something..." before he finished his sentence, Alton spotted Reese's slumped over dead body on the chair. "What happened to Reese? What the fuck is going on?" Alton asked, sounding like he was about to hyperventilate.

"Your cousin was the one that orchestrated all this bullshit to bring me down. He's the one that killed Tracy, Reese, Lance, Angie, Morgan and of course tried to murder me."

"Are you serious! I swear, Nico, I didn't know

nothing about it. You know my loyalty is to you. I would've never been a part of that bullshit. You have to believe me, Nico," Alton said sincerely.

"I do believe you, Alton."

"Oh good, man. I was worried for a minute," Alton said, easing up.

"I'll always have love for you, Alton, and it pains me to do this, but Reese is your family. I can't take the chance that your conscious will start fuckin' wit' you and you try to retaliate against me or you slip up and tell one of your family members and they choose to see revenge."

"Never that, Nico! I promise you, I won't say shit to nobody about this and I give you my word that I would never try to retaliate against you. I love you like a brother. I put that on everything."

"I love you like a brother too, but the thing is you're not my brother. Rest in peace, Alton." I then pulled the trigger ending his life. I closed my eyes for a second and there was only one thing I wanted to say, "God forgive me."

Chapter 19

Precious Cummings

5 Years Later...

"I think I'm in love," I said out loud when I laid eyes
on one of the sexiest women I had ever seen in my
life. The way the sun hit her butterscotch complex-
ion and the wind blew through her golden brown
hair as she strutted down 125th Street in Harlem
had a nigga open. She had to be one of the sexiest
women I had ever seen with her glossy lips, sen-
sual looks, and curvy figure. I watched her for a
few minutes before I decided to make my move. All
I wanted was her name. Five minutes later, I had
it. Precious Cummings. She didn't know it yet, but

Precious was going to be mine.

"Damn, nigga, you in an awfully good mood," Ritchie commented when I came through one of the blocks to check on some things. After all these years, I still felt like I had to be more hands on with shit after everything that had went down with Reese. He was this close to destroying everything I had worked so hard to build and I never wanted that shit to happen again. The only people left standing were Ritchie and I and together we running these streets and keeping the drug game on lock.

"I just got off the phone with this girl I've been seeing. She mad crazy, but in a good way."

"Well you know they say crazy women have the best pussy," Ritchie joked.

"I can attest to that being true, at least when it comes to Precious," I said thinking about how wet she felt the first time I slid inside. It was crazy because we had sex the night of our very first date and I wasn't expecting that. With her slick mouth and get money attitude, I figured she would've tried to make a nigga trick before giving up the panties, but I was wrong. But she played her cards right because I planned on doing more than trick on her. I was going to give her the world.

"So that's her name, Precious. She got any friends?" Ritchie questioned.

"Ain't you juggling enough women already."

"Can always make room for more, especially if she bad."

"I'll find out for you, but in the meantime how they handling business over here today? You know I had to come through and check on shit."

"It's all good. You know I be keeping these motherfuckers in check. I don't let shit slide," Ritchie said.

"Yeah, yeah, yeah don't go overboard now. But I was just passing through and since everything is good, I'ma go check on some of the other spots," I said getting back in my car.

"Cool. Don't forget to find out if yo' girl has a friend."

"I won't and call me if anything comes up." As I was driving to the next location my mind wandered to Precious. She was different then the other women I had been dating and the first woman that I knew I would eventually wife up. I dated and I even cared about a few chicks, but I didn't want to be tied down to any of them, but all that had changed.

"Yo, I've been sitting here waiting for you for over

an hour. Your phone going straight to voicemail, you can't pick up the phone and call a bitch, like what's really good?" Precious said when I arrived at her apartment.

"You still sexy as fuck even when you pissed. Sorry baby," I said leaning in to kiss her, but she stepped back. "What? I can't get a kiss?"

"Nope. I don't like waiting around for no mother-fuckin' body. Like my time is valuable."

"I understand. So, I'm an hour late. How much time is that worth?"

"Maybe like a g. Actually more, but a g will suffice." I pulled out 10 one hundred dollar bills and handed them to her.

"Now can I have a kiss?"

"Nope. That g only made up for the hour you had me waiting. I'm still mad. Why was your phone off and why didn't you call me?"

"Honestly, my cell died. I've been running around all day. The car I'm in, I just got it, and I still haven't gotten a car charger. What more can I say but that I'm sorry. The whole day I was dealing wit' bullshit and there was only one thing that kept me smiling."

"What's that?"

"Knowing I was gonna see you."

"Word?"

"Word."

"I guess you can get a kiss then," Precious said, placing her soft lips on mine. I positioned my hand behind her neck pulling her in even closer. The scent of the perfume she was wearing though unintentional was seducing me. I was ready to skip our date and instead lay her down and make love. But Precious was dressed for a night out and I knew she was ready to go, especially after waiting for over an hour.

"You sure you want to go out?" I whispered in her ear.

"Do you not see this fuckin' dress I got on? Oh you taking me out and someplace super nice too. Now let's go," she hissed, grabbing her purse.

"You gets no argument from me. I can't lie, you look exceptional tonight."

"I'm glad you noticed. I did it for you. From what I've been hearing in the streets, Nico Carter is that nigga. I just wanna represent. Let motherfuckers out here know, you have great taste across the board." Precious playfully winked her eye.

"So you representing for me now?"

"You tell me, am I?"

"I don't know if you ready for all that," I remarked.

"What you mean by that?" She frowned as I opened the passenger car door for her.

"Are you getting in?" I laughed after she stood outside the car, not moving.

"Not until you answer my question."

"Real talk, I've never had a girlfriend in my life and there's a reason for that. I'm a complicated dude and to be my woman requires a lot. I've never met a woman that I felt qualified for the position."

"You mean you never met a woman that qualified until me," Precious said without hesitation before getting in the car. I couldn't help but smile because that was one of the reasons I was so drawn to Precious—her cocky, confident attitude.

"Is this place nice enough?" I asked when we entered the upscale restaurant on the Upper East Side.

"This place is sexy, sophisticated, and has a little edge to it... definitely a good look."

"I thought it was a good fit. Reminded me of you." The soaring ceilings and garden windows created a grand setting that I knew would fit her taste. She liked for things to be a little over the top, but not overwhelming, which described this place perfectly. As the hostess showed us to the table, I watched Precious walking. I loved how she was such a feisty hood chick, but yet she fit in perfectly with the ambiance.

"Baby, are we poppin' bottles of champagne or what," she stated after the hostess left.

"Whatever you want."

"Is that only for tonight or always?" She smirked.

"That depends on how you play the game."

"Oh so we playing a game now? You shoulda

said that from jump so I could've been wearing my poker face."

"I thought you already was."

"I don't know whether to be flattered or offended by your comment."

"I was thinking... why don't you move in with me?"

"Excuse me! My fault, I didn't mean to say that so loud but umm, you caught me completely off guard. Less than an hour ago you was telling me you wasn't sure if I was ready to represent you now you're asking me to move in. Like what the fuck."

"I never said I wasn't ready, I said I wasn't sure if you were. I wanted you from the moment I saw you walking down 125th Street."

"Really?"

"You say that like you don't believe me."

"I guess I don't. I mean I def think you want me, but wanting somebody physically and asking them to move in is two different things."

"Maybe I'm moving fast." I shrugged.

"Maybe? We've only been on a handful of dates," Precious pointed out.

'True, but what about all those hours we spent on the phone talking, getting to know each other. Or the night we went on our first date and afterwards we chilled at the park and I opened up to you about my childhood and how I became the man I am today. Or later on that night you put it on me like you wanted to own it."

"Let's go for it. What we got to lose," Precious said leaning over the table to kiss me.

"I was hoping you would say that."

"I can't believe I'm moving in to Nico Carter's brownstone in Brooklyn Heights. I am truly moving on up in the world." She giggled. "Have the waitress bring out the champagne so we can celebrate."

"Before we start getting drunk on love, I want you to really understand what you're jumping into. We about to make a serious leap and once we do there's no turning back."

"I don't want to turn back. I'm all in. I'm sure you got some shit wit' you, but hell so do I. I'll be true to you and as long as you stay true to me then life will be sweet."

I took Precious's hand and stroked her slender fingers. It was the first time I looked at a woman's hand imagining putting a ring on it. I knew I was probably moving too fast because although we shared a lot of our deepest thoughts and the sex was amazing, there was a lot I didn't know about her. What I did know was I wanted Precious Cummings to be my woman and that trumped all my hesitation.

Chapter 20

Caught Out There

It seemed from the moment I laid eyes on Precious our relationship went from zero to sixty in record setting speed. I normally moved with caution and preferred to take things slowly, but with her, I threw caution to the wind and jumped right out the window. Honestly, it had me scratching my head sometimes, but once she got settled in my crib it felt right.

"So what you got planned for the day?" Precious asked, sitting up in bed.

"Regular shit. I'm considering investing in this club in Queens so I'm going by there to check shit out. Other than that same ole' thing."

"Are we still going out with Ritchie and Inga

this weekend?"

"Oh, I forgot about that. So things must be going a'ight wit' them, huh?"

"From what Inga said, it is. Why, Ritchie saying something different?"

"I haven't talked to Ritchie about Inga since we first hooked them up and he said he was feeling her."

"But that was months ago," Precious said, looking puzzled.

"I know that. I stay out of relationship shit, especially when it comes to Ritchie," I said buttoning up my shirt.

"Why, because he be fucking wit' mad bitches?"

"I don't know what that man do wit' his dick and as long as he ain't touching nothing of mine, I don't care and neither should you."

"Inga, my girl. You know I gotta look out for her."

"Then school her ass. If he ain't yo' nigga he don't owe you shit so do you and even if he is yo' nigga still do you, just in case you need to bounce."

"So wait. You sayin' I should be doing me instead always waitin' around on you?" Precious asked.

"Babe, I ain't the typical nigga. You ain't gon' neva wanna bounce and I'm not gon' let you anyway." I smiled.

"So if you do some fucked up shit and I'm ready

to cut you off, you gon' what, hold me hostage." She laughed.

"Exactly. I'll keep yo' ass tied up in this bedroom until you come to your senses."

"You are so crazy."

"Yep, crazy about you. Now let me get outta here. Call me if you need me."

"You do the same." She grinned. Wait!" Precious shouted when I was almost out the door.

"What's up?" I asked, coming back in the bedroom.

"You not gon' leave me nothing? You know I'm about to hit these streets."

"I just hit you off heavy the other day."

"Baby, that shit been spent. What can I say, I have expensive taste."

"That's another reason why I know you ain't going nowhere. I got you so spoiled, can't nobody else afford you... here," I said dropping a wad a cash on the bed.

"Thank you, baby," I heard her yell out.

"Just make sure you buy something sexy to wear for me tonight," I yelled back.

"I was beginning to think you wasn't coming," Marshawn said when I finally arrived at the club.

"Man, I had so much going on today. I got here as soon as I could. This a nice spot you got here," I said, looking around before following Marshawn to the back of the club. It had a sexy high-end atmosphere. The interior was lush yet cozy with three bars, leather banquettes, elevated dance floor, metal DJ booth, secluded alcoves, and exposed brick with elegant chandeliers.

"Thank you. I've put everything into this club and business is really booming, but it cost money to run a business, promote, pay to get the hottest artist, and with my business partner gone, this overhead is taking me under," Marshawn admitted.

"It's messed up what happened to Malcolm. I didn't know him that well, but he seemed like a good dude."

"He was. The crazy part is I was supposed to be in the car with him, but at the last minute something came up and I had to stay here. That could've been me killed in that accident too."

"I feel you man that's why you gotta always count your blessings and live life to the fullest. You never know when your time is up."

"True dat. That's why I love living mine in this club. It comes with headaches, but I also have a lot of fun."

"I feel you."

"When we met last week, we went over the numbers and your share of the profits, but you wanted to come by and look at the place before making a final decision. So what do you think?"

"I think I would definitely like to be a partner. I like the location. As I said, this spot is nice, much nicer than what you described. I'm impressed."

"Does that mean we have a deal?"

"Yep, we have a deal," I said shaking Marshawn's hand.

"Let's have a drink. You know, a toast to our new partnership," he suggested.

"I have someplace I need to be, but I guess one drink wouldn't hurt."

"Porscha, pour me the usual, but make it two. "I want you to meet my new partner. This is Nico Carter."

"It's a pleasure. Your name rings bells out here in these streets," she said smiling.

"Porscha is our most popular bartender," Marshawn said taking his drink.

"I can believe that. Pretty girl, pretty smile," I said.

"Thank you," she said shyly. I could see she was blushing so she put her head down while pouring my drink. "Here you go," she said finally looking back up with a sweet smile across her face. There was something I definitely liked about Porscha.

"Baby, these diamond earrings are beautiful. Thank you," Precious said leaning over the table and giving me a kiss. "Last week you bought that incredible diamond tennis bracelet, now these earrings. If I didn't know better I would think you had a guilty conscious about something." I sat there with a blank stare on my face. "It was a joke, Nico, lighten up." She laughed.

"I know you was jokin'. That was my poker face."

"Oh really." Precious smiled as she took off her earrings to put on her new diamond studs. "So I was thinking we could go to the movies tonight. Inga was telling me about some new movie she saw with Ritchie and it's supposed to be really good."

"I would babe, but I have to stop by the club tonight."

"Ever since you became a partner in that club, you're always there. I thought you said you were more like an investor and you wouldn't be dealing with the day to day operations?"

"I am, but I have to check on my investment. Make sure shit is running properly. I don't want them running through my money and not maintaining shit properly."

"I suppose."

"I'll make it up to you, baby. We can go to the movies tomorrow and do whatever else you want to do."

"I guess that means we'll be going on a shopping spree. Fifth Avenue here we come."

"You know I love you."

"You better," she smacked.

"I don't get an I love you too?"

"I love you too, Nico."

I did love Precious and me fucking Porscha didn't taint that one bit, I thought to myself as I watched Porscha in action. "How does that feel baby," she purred between deep throating my dick.

"You doing it just right," I said stroking Porscha's hair as I watched her wet lips massage my tool. Her dick sucking skills were excellent. She had some good pussy too, but it was her head game that had me dealing with Porscha on a regular. After that day Marshawn introduced her at the bar, the next few times I came through, she would flirt with me and I would entertain it. It took me a couple months before I actually decided to deal with her on that level because I wanted to make sure she wasn't one of those stalker type chicks.

Everybody knew Precious was wifey and I didn't need nobody fuckin' up our happy home. So I had to be extremely careful about how I moved. Porscha was the first chick that I messed around on Precious with and I had no intention of making it a regular thing. I knew eventually it would come to an end and I hope Porscha did too.

"I gotta go," I said after finishing things up with Porscha.

"But we just finished having sex. Can't you lay with me for a little while?" she asked patting the spot next to her on the bed.

"Do I ever lay with you after we have sex," I stated as I was getting dressed.

"We've been messing around for a few months now, I thought things might change."

"Nothing has changed, but if you push things they might."

"I'm not trying to push things, Nico, but I know you must be developing some sort of feelings for me. I can feel it when we're making love."

"Listen, Porscha," I said, sitting down on the edge of the bed. "You see where we're at, we're in a hotel room. This ain't my crib and you're not my girl. Precious is the only woman I make love to. I enjoy your company. You're a sweet girl, but that feeling you said you get from me when we're making love, is just me enjoying the sex, nothing more."

"That's cold, Nico."

"We both grown and I'm not gon' sugar coat shit for you. If you can't handle the situation the way it is right now then let me know so we can end things because it ain't gon' change. This is what it is."

"I can handle things. I'm not gonna lie, I did think there was a chance of things getting more serious between us. I mean, I have genuine feelings for you. But you were always upfront about having a girl so it is what it is. If this is how it has to be, then I can deal with it," Porscha finally said, after sitting on the bed quiet for a few minutes.

"Okay," I kissed her on the forehead. "Go buy yourself something nice," I said, leaving some money on the nightstand like I always did. I didn't leave Porscha money because I thought of her as a prostitute because I did care about her. I left her money because I thought everyone should be paid for their services and Porscha was providing a service.

When I got home later on that night Precious was lying peacefully in the bed. She looked so beautiful, almost angelic. I took a shower and got in the bed completely exhausted. I had been running around all day and coming home and going to sleep had been the one thing I was looking forward to.

"I was calling you all night, but your phone kept going to voicemail," Precious said before I even had a chance to close my eyes.

"Babe, my phone died in the club and I didn't have a charger."

"Nico, are you fuckin' around on me?" she asked point blank.

"Why would you ask me that?"

"Because for the last few weeks, things have seemed off and my gut is telling me that you fuckin' around. My gut is usually always right. But a bitch wanna be wrong 'cause if I'm not..." her voice trailed off.

"Baby, I've had a long day and night. I'm tired. Can't we talk about this in the morning."

"If you ain't fuckin' around then the conversation don't have to be that long, unless the answer is yes. If that's the case, then you need to wake the fuck up."

"The answer is no."

"No what?"

"No, I'm not fuckin' around on you, Precious. I love you... goodnight." I wasn't sure if Precious believed me or not, but what could I do? Tell her truth? No good would come from that. Plus, I was never going to let her go. It was 'til death do us part.

Chapter 21

She Loves Me, She Loves Me Not

Ritchie and I were out of town handling business when I got the phone call that seemed to be the beginning of my life spinning out of control. "Porscha, I'm in the middle of something. Let me call you back," I said about to hang up until I realized she was crying.

"Nico, I swear it wasn't my fault," she mumbled between sniffles. "She jumped on me and just went crazy."

"Who jumped on you?"

"Your girlfriend."

"Precious jumped on you? Hold up, tell me exactly what happened."

"This happened like an hour ago. I was at the club with my cousin and a friend. They knew the girl she was with and my cousin introduced me to her. Then she just came at me asking was I fucking her man. I was like, who is your man and she said Nico Carter. I told her I wasn't, but she didn't believe me. She swung a champagne bottle at me. Luckily, my cousin knocked it away before it hit me, but then Precious jumped on me and started punching me and wouldn't stop. The shit was a fuckin' nightmare," she cried.

"Where is Precious at now?"

"I don't know, security made her leave. They said I should call the police and press charges."

"Don't do that shit, Porscha. You understand? Do you understand?" I barked again when she didn't answer the first time.

"Yeah, I understand. I won't press charges, but I'm only doing it for you, Nico."

"A'ight. I'll call you when I get back in town." The second I hung up with Porscha I called Precious. "Answer your fuckin' phone," I yelled out loud in frustration when it kept ringing and then going to voicemail. I knew she saw it was me and was ignoring my call.

"Is everything okay?" Ritchie questioned, when I got back in the car.

"No. Some shit went down with Precious. I

gotta get back home."

"But we haven't finished handling our business here."

"You can stay and finish. I trust you can handle this shit. But I gotta go."

"Man, is she worth it?" Ritchie huffed.

"Excuse me?" I questioned with a raised eyebrow.

"I'm just saying. Ever since I've known you, you've always put business first. Now this chick got you breakin' out early before we've gotten our shit handled. That ain't the Nico I know."

"Precious ain't some chick, she's my woman. And business is being dealt with, that's what I got you for. And I'm the same Nico, so don't come at me like that again," I said before driving off.

The entire time I was on my way back to New York I thought about how I was going to come at Precious. She still wasn't answering my calls so I knew she was pissed. I wasn't sure how this was going to unfold so I decided to play it by ear. When I arrived to the crib it was the middle of the afternoon, but Precious was still in bed asleep.

"Baby, are you okay?" She shrugged her arm as if wanting me to get out of her face, but I continued.

"I came home as soon as I heard what happened."

"I'm fine. You need to go check on yo' bitch."

"Precious, what are you talking about?"

"Don't play wit' me, Nico. I know all about you and Porscha. That's why yo' phone always be going to voicemail 'cause you laying up wit' that bitch. Nigga, fuck you." She pulled the blankets over her head as if she was going back to sleep.

I grabbed the covers and threw them on the floor. "I told you about that slick-ass mouth of yours," I said, pointing my finger at her. By the crazed look on her face it was obvious that pissed her the fuck off. She was now wide awake and seemed ready for a battle.

"I don't give a fuck whether you like what is coming out my mouth or not. You running round here fucking that cunt, and then the dumb bitch wanna step to me at the club. You lucky I didn't kill the bitch."

"Precious, I'm not fucking that girl. I barely know the chick. Whatever she told you was a lie."

"Nico, you must think you dealing wit' a straight fool. Who's the one that called you about the fight I was in?"

I paused for a minute because her question caught me off guard. "Inga called Ritchie and told him, and then he told me," I said, quickly coming up with an answer off the top of my head that sounded plausible.

Precious just nodded her head as she walked

over to her purse and retrieved her cell phone.

"Who you calling?" I asked.

"Inga. I'ma ask her if she called Ritchie and told him what happened."

I grabbed the phone out of her hand, so she went and picked up the cordless and I grabbed that too.

"What the fuck you need to call Inga for? There is no reason to get her in the middle of our shit."

"Bitch, you put her in the middle. You know damn well you didn't find out from Ritchie. That trifling Porscha called you crying the blues, and that's how yo' lyin' ass found out what happened. I'm done wit' yo' punk-ass. Go be wit' her, 'cause I won't have no problem replacing yo' bitch ass."

I grabbed Precious by her throat and slammed her against the wall. I could feel my eyes bulging and beads of sweat gathering on my forehead.

"If you trying to instill fear in me, the shit ain't working. I could really give a fuck. Nigga you's a clown as far as I was concerned," Precious spit at me full of rage.

"Precious, first of all get all that leaving and being with the next man out of your head. We family now. It's 'til death do us part. How many times do I have to tell you that? I'm sorry I had to grab on you like this, but you was flying off the handle, and I need your full attention. Baby, I'm sorry. I did fuck around with that girl, Porscha, but it was only a couple of times, nothing serious. She was out of line for even crossing your path, let alone saying a word to you, and she will be dealt with accordingly. But, Precious, you can't let these scandalous hoes come in and ruin our happy home. They just jealous and sitting around waiting and plotting to take your place. You smarter than that. You can't let that happen. I'm going to let go of your neck, but you have to promise me that you'll calm down and be mature about this shit."

She nodded her head yes to let me know she wouldn't black out on me when I let her go.

"So what you want me to do, Nico? Act like didn't nothing happen between you and that bitch?"

"Precious, I know that's easier said than done, but I'm begging you to be the bigger person and let it go. I promise I won't fuck with her ever again. I made a mistake. I'm a man. I can admit that. I'm asking for your forgiveness. I promise I'll make it up to you."

"You sound sincere, but the damage has been done," she said calmly.

"I can undo the damage. You know you love me and I love you, too. Let me make it up to you baby, please," I begged. I didn't want to lose her and in my heart I believed she felt the same way.

"Okay, I'll let you make it up to me, but you better not fuck up again, Nico," Precious warned, before getting in bed and going right back to sleep.

I spent the next few months doing everything I could to prove to Precious that I deserved her forgiveness. I bought her the new Benz she had been begging me to get her, took her to LA so she could go shopping on Rodeo Drive, and finally I took her on a vacation to Antigua and proposed. The five-carat rock sealed the deal. Precious accepted my marriage proposal and our relationship was finally back on track or at least it seemed to be.

"Where you going?" I asked Precious as she was grabbing her car keys to leave.

"To have drinks with my girl Tina."

"You've been going out a lot lately."

"No I haven't... maybe a little bit. I've been enjoying showing off my ridiculous rock." Precious smiled, flashing her finger.

"It does look good on you. Enjoy yourself, but don't be out too late."

"I won't. Bye babe," she said giving me a kiss. As I watched Precious leave I couldn't help but feel that something was slightly off. She was saying all the right things and on the surface we seemed to be more in love than ever. I wasn't able to put my finger on it so I brushed it off as me overanalyzing shit. Before I could think about it any further I saw that Ritchie was calling me.

"What's up?"

"I was calling to see if you were still interested in meeting with that new diesel connect I got?"

"Definitely, but like I said I want to start with a small order. See how shit moves on the street and then move forward from there."

"Cool, I'll set that up."

"A'ight, let me know when," I said before getting off the phone with Ritchie. Ritchie was another one that had seemed off for the last few weeks. He was coming up missing all the time and slacking on business, but lately he seemed to have snapped out of whatever funk he was in and was back handling shit like he was supposed to. With this potential new drug connect we had an excellent opportunity to make a shit load of money which made me respect Ritchie for getting his shit together and coming through.

Chapter 22

From Bad To Worse

When I woke up and started my day, if someone had said my night was going to end like this I would've said they were a motherfuckin' lie. It all started with a phone call.

"What's up, baby?" I said when I answered the phone.

"I was calling to tell you bye," Precious replied.

"What you mean, 'bye'? Where you going?"

"I can't do this no more, Nico."

"Do what? Stop talking in riddles, Precious."

"After we got back from Antigua I tried to put the whole Porscha situation behind me, but I couldn't. The only person that was able to console me was Ritchie."

"What the fuck did you say?"

"Nico, I've been seeing Ritchie for a few months now, and we're in love. I'm pregnant and the baby is his," she said with a slight sniffle in her voice as if holding back tears.

"Precious, don't fucking play with me. This shit ain't funny."

"It's not meant to be. I've packed my stuff. I'm leaving you."

"Where the fuck are you right now?"

"On my way to Ritchie's."

"I'm going to give you one more chance to take all this bullshit back before I lose it."

"I can't take it back, Nico, 'cause it's the truth. Why do you think Ritchie was showing you so much shade? He couldn't stand the fact that I refused to leave you. But once I found out I was pregnant, I decided it was time to let you go."

"That might be my seed. How you know I'm not the father?"

"I just know," she said, sounding confident.

"Then you a dead bitch," I said and hung up the phone. I bypassed my original destination and did a quick U-turn heading toward Ritchie's house. I knew shit had seemed shaky with Precious, but never did I expect this. I kept glancing down at my phone knowing that any second Precious was going to call me back saying this was all a bad joke, but that call never came.

When I pulled up to Ritchie's house I saw Precious' car parked across the street. I kicked the fuck out of that shit before running up the stairs and knocking on the front door.

"Nico... umm what are you doing here?" Ritchie questioned, looking shocked.

"Where the fuck is Precious!" I barked with my gun in hand.

"Yo, what's wrong wit' you and why would Precious be over here?"

"Nigga, kill that bullshit! Precious called me not too long ago saying you all been fucking and ya in love and having a baby together."

Ritchie seemed to be in complete shock. He was standing in his living room not saying shit, just standing there with a dumb ass look on his face.

"Man, I don't know what type of game Precious is playing, but ain't nothing going on between us. She's not here, I swear man."

"Don't play wit' me, Ritchie," I said, cocking the gun and putting it to his head. "If you tell me the truth, I'll let you live, but if you continue to lie, you a dead motherfucker."

"I wanted to tell you, but Precious begged me not to. It was an accident. She came on to me and I got caught up. I'm sorry, man. But this 'we're in love and having a baby,' I don't know where none of that is coming from. Precious must be tryna hurt you 'cause of that Porscha situation."

"We supposed to be brothers. We grew up together. We lost our entire crew because of betrayal.

Never did I believe you would betray me too. I hope fuckin' my woman was worth yo' life," I said before blasting Ritchie's brains out. By the time I did a quick search of his house making sure Precious wasn't there, police were surrounding Ritchie's crib. All I could do was shake my head and say, "This bitch set me up."

As I sat in my jail cell, I kept replaying the last few months, trying to figure out how I didn't see this shit coming. I had dealt with the most ruthless criminals on the streets and couldn't none of them take me down, never did I think a scheming bitch would and that's exactly what happened to me. My attorney informed me that an anonymous female caller had tipped police off about the shooting at Ritchie's house. I knew that was nobody but Precious. I wondered at what point did she start plotting my demise. Did she ever forgive me for cheating with Porscha or was this her plan all along. She played the game like a pro because I was in jail facing first-degree murder charges for a double homicide. Come to find out a dude named Butch was killed right outside of Ritchie's house. My gut was telling me that Precious had something to do with that too.

"Tommy, man, did you go by the house and get that for me?" I asked one of my only workers that I trusted, when he came for a jail visit.

"It wasn't there."

"What you mean it wasn't there?" I asked, thinking maybe I was hearing Tommy incorrectly.

"The duffel bag was gone. The million wasn't there," he repeated.

"Precious took my fuckin' money."

"That's not all she took."

"What do you mean?"

"Her clothes, shoes, purses, jewelry, and your jewelry too."

"I should've learned from my mother that you can't trust no woman," I said shaking my head. "Remember that apartment Precious had in Harlem?"

"Sure do."

"She doesn't know that I know, but she kept it. I want you to put two men on it. She might be hiding out there with my money."

"If we find her do you want us..." I knew what Tommy was asking without him saying it.

"No. You leave that for me," I made clear. Precious would pay with her life for what she did to me, but I would be the one to end it.

"Nico, we requested a speedy trial so we need to start preparing for trial," my attorney said as I was halfway listening to him. I was still pissed that I was denied bail and I would have to sit in a jail cell while I awaited trial. The crazy part was that after all the dirt I had done in the streets since I was a teenager, I had never been to jail until now. "Nico are you listening to me? I know you're probably scared but..."

"I ain't neva scared," I said cutting my attorney off. "The worst thing that can happen is that I'm found guilty. But with the amount of money I'm paying you, you'll find a loophole to get me off on appeal. I'm charged with killing two drug dealers. When all the hype dies down, won't nobody give a fuck."

"I will do my best to get a not guilty verdict or at the very least a hung jury."

"Do what you have to do. There's a phone call I need to make so I'll see you tomorrow," I said to my attorney so I could go make my phone call.

"Nico, I was waiting for you to call me." I could hear Porscha smiling through the phone when she answered. I had cut her off, but when all this shit went down and I needed someone on the outside to keep me in the loop, she was there for me as if I had never walked out her life.

"Listen, I need you to do something for me."

"Sure, what is it, baby?"

"I need you to get in touch with Inga."

"You talking about Precious' friend?"

"Yes. I want you to let her know that Ritchie was fuckin' Precious behind both of our backs and that Precious is pregnant with his baby." I highly doubted the last part was true, but Inga didn't need to know that.

"Precious scandalous ass was fuckin' Ritchie. I knew she was a skeeze," Porscha said, sounding happy that she had some foul information about Precious.

"Then I want you to tell Inga I'll be in touch with her."

"I'm on it, baby."

"'Good, I'll be in touch."

As expected I was found guilty of all charges. The way the DA was gunning for me I wasn't surprised, but I wasn't worried either. I hated being caged up like an animal, but I knew in my heart that I would see the outside of these prison walls again and a lot sooner than anybody thought.

Even after the guilty verdict I was in touch with Inga as she had become somewhat of a street informant for me. After finding out about Ritchie and Precious, she was more than willing to try and bring Precious down. Inga had informed me that

Tommy had turned on me. He was trying to keep the million dollars for himself. Somehow him, Boogie—whom Precious used to work for—and his nephews all ended up dead. The money was never found. That meant Precious still had it and I figured those deaths were linked to her. Inga had even been in touch with Precious a few times, but she would never give Inga her location as if she knew her best friend had now become the enemy. I needed an update, but it seemed Inga had went ghost and I wanted to know why.

"Hello," a girl answered whose voice I didn't recognize.

"Can I speak to Porscha," I said, hoping Porscha could tell me if she had heard or seen Inga.

"Umm, Porsha ain't here."

"Do you know when she'll be back?"

"She ain't coming back."

"Who is this? What you mean she ain't coming back?" I questioned, confused by that response. "I spoke to her a month or so ago and she didn't say anything about leaving town."

"Nico, this is Porscha's cousin, Olivia. There is no easy way to say this. Porscha was killed a couple weeks ago."

"What... by who?"

"We don't know. She was found dead with another girl named Inga."

"Inga too... damn."

"You knew Inga?"

"Yeah, I did. I'm sorry about your cousin. Give Porscha's family my condolences," I said before hanging up. This shit was crazy. I knew for a fact Precious was behind the deaths of Porscha and Inga, but yet she was running around with my motherfuckin' money, free as a bird. I hope she was enjoying it because before I took my last breath, Precious Cummings would pay in blood for what she did to me.

Chapter 23

Against All Odds

Two Years Later...

The streets had counted me out and left me to rot in prison, but a nigga like me was built for this shit. Like I knew he would, my high priced attorney was able to get me off on a technicality. The DA's office didn't even want to spend the time or money to re-try the case, instead they gave me time served and my walking papers. I was a free man with a to do list and killing Precious was at the top of it.

Many things changed while I had been locked up. Precious was now married to a superstar rap-per named Supreme. She was living every hood girls dream. She went from a project girl living in Brooklyn to being the queen of the streets as my woman and now the first lady of the biggest rapper out, but none of that would protect her from me. While I was locked up most had counted me out, but a few stayed loyal and was keeping tabs on Precious for me. Before she got married and was living on an estate she shared an apartment in Edgewater, New Jersey with a girl named Rhonda. I decided to pay her a visit.

"Hi, can I help you with something," a semi cute girl with a bubbly personality answered the door and said.

"I hope so. I'm old friend of Precious."

"Oh, Precious doesn't live here anymore."

"I know, Rhonda. That is your name... right?"

She gave me this baffled look. "How did you know my name and why..." Before she could say another word, I grabbed Rhonda by her throat and dragged her into the apartment with a gun to her head. I slammed the door shut and then put the gun to my mouth, motioning her to keep quiet.

"I'm going to release my hand from around your throat, but if you scream I will blow your brains out. Do you understand?"

She nodded her head yes as tears began to run down her face. "Why are you doing this?" she asked in a low voice, breathing hard.

"Because Precious did some fucked up shit

to me and it's time for her to deal with the consequences."

"I don't know anything about that," she cried.

"That might be true, but unfortunately for
you Precious got you involved the day you became
roommates."

"But she doesn't live here anymore."

"I know, but you're still friends. I want you to
call Precious right now and tell her you need for
her to come over."

"She's out of town, she won't be able to come
over."

"I see we're going to have to do this the hard
way, Rhonda."

"Wait! I'm telling you the truth."

"No, you're lying. Precious is not out of town.
Do you want to try this again? This is your last
chance."

"Please, don't do this," she pleaded. Precious
is my friend. I can't call and lure her to her death. I
wouldn't be able to live with myself."

"Have it your way," I said knocking her over
the over the head with the butt of my gun. I then
pulled her limp body into her bedroom, tying her
arms and wrist to each bedpost. I put duct tape
over her mouth. A few minutes after I was finished
she began to come to. She was mumbling so I lifted
the tape from her mouth.

"I don't want to die," she muttered.

"Then call Precious," I said, holding up her cell

phone. She shook her head no. "You're willing to die for your so-called friend. I hate to break it to you, but Precious has no loyalty to nobody but herself. Now make the call," I demanded.

"I can't do it knowing that you plan on hurting her. I think you're trying to scare me. I don't think you would really kill me. Please just go. I won't say anything about what happened."

"You must not know who I am. But that's cool. Honestly, I really don't need you. I know where Precious lives. I figured it would be easier to get her to this apartment then going to her crib. Guess I was wrong. I should've gone to her house first because now I have to kill you anyway."

"No! No!" Rhonda screamed out before I put the tape back over her mouth. I grabbed a pillow from behind her and placed it over her face to muzzle the sound of the bullet to her head when I pulled trigger. After Rhonda was dead I immediately got in my car and headed to the estate where Precious lived with her husband.

When I pulled up to the winding driving, there was no security at the front and the gate was open. It was as if the stars were aligned in my favor. I decided to park my car on the side of the road and walk up. When I got to the top of the hill, I noticed Precious getting out of her car.

"You've done very well for yourself. I'm proud of you, Precious." She closed her eyes as if she didn't believe I was real. "Baby, open your eyes. I'm not going anywhere. I'm the real deal."

"Nico, you can't be real."

"Precious, you're just as beautiful, if not more, than the first time I saw you walking the streets of Harlem. I knew you didn't belong there. Now look at you, married to a superstar, living in a mansion.

"You made Brooklyn proud. But as much as you cleaned yourself up, you still have those dark eyes just like me. Remember I told you besides me and my father you were the only other person I ever met with the same darkness in your eyes. That right there should've been enough incentive for me to let you walk away that day, but instead I wanted you more. Because of that, I had to pay the price for my decision. Now it's time for you to pay the price for yours."

"Nico, please. I was so immature back then and I made a mistake. But I'm a different person now. I've put the streets behind me and turned my life around."

"It's all good that you turned your life around, but you had to give my soul to the devil in order to get it. Not once did you think about the life you took away from me, and the money you stole. You destroyed everything we had over some pussy. A bitch I didn't even give a fuck about.

"But that didn't matter to you, because you're

like me. Your pride and your ego dictate your moves. But, Precious, with every decision you make in life, there are consequences. And your consequence is death."

"Nico, don't. What can I do to stop this? I don't want to die."

"You're already dead. I just came to take it in blood. But because I still have mad love for you Precious, I won't make you suffer the way I did your friend."

"What friend?"

"If I'm not mistaken her name was Rhonda," I said with a devious chuckle that I knew she would detest.

"You killed Rhonda, but why?"

"I really didn't want to take the chance and come here to kill you. I wasn't sure what type of security you were working with, but obviously not enough," he said, glancing around the estate. "So I paid her an unexpected visit.

"All I asked her to do was get you over to the apartment, and I would handle the rest, but she refused. She was a true friend to the end unlike Inga."

"Nico, hasn't there been enough death in our lives? I can give you back the million dollars and more, if you like. I have a husband, Nico, and I'm pregnant with his child. I'm living the life I never dreamed possible. Don't take that away from me."

"I came back to take what's mine, and that's your life." Not for one second did I believe Precious was pregnant. She was lying just like she lied about being pregnant by Ritchie knowing I would kill him. Once again, Precious was trying to scheme and manipulate her way out of trouble, but it wasn't going to work. Her luck had finally run out. I raised my gun, and we both turned when we heard a car pulling up.

As the car got closer, I could see what looked to be Supreme inside. He jumped out and his bodyguards followed with guns raised.

But it was too late. The loud explosion ripped through Precious' chest. The pressure jolted her back, and she hit her car before falling down to the ground. I started shooting in the direction of Supreme and his bodyguards as I ran vanishing in the darkness.

Chapter 24

On The Run

After shooting Precious and leaving her for dead I went on the run. I was determined not to go back to prison no matter what the cost. I soon learned that Precious survived the shooting, but after she was released and was leaving the hospital, her and Supreme were ambushed with gunshots. Once again Precious survived, but Supreme was pronounced dead at the scene.

During my time on the run I had reached out to a girl named Nina. She used to be a drug carrier for me and we also had a sexual relationship. Nina always wanted it to be more serious, but I wasn't checkin' for her like that. The good thing was she still was down for a nigga and when I needed her she was there.

"Nina, thank you for everything you've done for me," I said standing in the kitchen about to eat some Chinese food she had brought home for me. Nina let me stay at an apartment she had in Manhattan. It was nothing fancy, but comfortable and clean. Most importantly, it was no place anybody would think about coming to look for me.

"Nico, you know I would do anything for you. I'm just glad you trusted me enough to call and ask for my help."

"You were always loyal and with everything I was going through that's what I needed."

"I still can't believe all the bullshit Precious put you through. Because of her your life got fucked up. She need to pay for that shit," Nina snapped.

"Nina, I wanna put all that shit behind me."

"What you mean put it behind you?"

"There is no doubt Precious did the ultimate foul shit to me, but she's suffered enough. Her husband is dead and come to find out when I shot her, she really was pregnant so she lost her baby too. The fact that I'm responsible for Precious losing her baby is still eatin' me up. I want to put all this shit behind me and move on and after you make this final drop for me I'll have enough money to do that."

"You're leaving town?" Nina asked sounding panicked.

"I told you from day one that after I got enough money up I was outta here. New York is way too hot for me."

"Where will you go?"

"Either down south or the West Coast. I'm still deciding."

"I'll come with you," Nina proposed.

"Nina, I can't ask you to do that."

"You don't have to ask. I want to come."

"But your family and friends are all here. I don't want you putting you life on hold to go on the run with me," I said, thinking be giving up a lot.

"I want my life to be with you. I don't care about that other stuff. We never had a chance to make it work in the past. Maybe in a new state we can have a fresh start. Who wants to be on the run alone? You know I'll make a great partner." Nina smiled.

Nina did make a valid point. It would be nice to have someone by my side that I could trust while dodging the police. She had already proven to be an asset. When I got out of jail I had a connect set up to get back in the drug game, but after my confrontation with Precious didn't go as planned, I had to go underground. I couldn't afford to miss out on the opportunity to make some money and that was one of the main reasons I reached out to Nina. She had been in the drug game before working for me so she knew how to move. She handled my business since I wasn't able to show my face and it paid off. Last few months I had stacked enough money to get out of New York for good.

"You've convinced me. I guess we'll be leaving this motherfucker together," I said.

"Yes! You won't regret it," Nina beamed, wrapping her arms around me and giving me a hug. "I need to go and take care of some things. Do you need anything before I leave?"

"No, I'm straight. After that deal goes down tomorrow, I'm trying to be out a couple days after that. Will you be ready by then?"

"I'll be ready. I don't want you to have any excuses for leaving me behind. See you soon," Nina said before heading out.

As I lay in bed before I was about to take a shower, I started reflecting on the rollercoaster ride my life had been on. Then I thought about how I had been hauled up in this apartment for the last few months but it was better then being locked up in a 6x8 jail cell. It was time for me to move on and I was ready.

When I got out the shower, I threw on some sweatpants and sat down on the couch to watch television. The TV was on, but my mind hadn't stopped wondering. I was so caught up in my thoughts that I didn't even notice that I had company.

"Long time no see," Precious said, sneaking up

on me with a nine-millimeter pointing directly at my head.

My eyes remained fixed on her, and I didn't flinch even with death staring me in the face. "My lovely Precious. I knew we'd meet again."

"I'm sure you did, just not under these circumstances."

"What do you mean by that?"

"Save the bullshit, Nico. Not in my worst nightmare did I believe you would come back and kill my husband. I can understand you seeking revenge on me and tryna end my life because I tried to end yours first by setting you up on that murder charge. I'll take that as settling the score, even though because of your actions I also lost my unborn child. That was foul. But to then come back and blaze Supreme while we're leaving the hospital. For that you gotta die."

I let out a deep sigh and shook my head. I put my hands over my mouth and rubbed my chin thinking about everything Precious had said.

She stepped back a little bit while keeping her finger firmly on the trigger.

"We've both done some fucked up shit to one another, but I swear on everything I've ever loved, which includes you, I ain't kill Supreme. And honestly, when you said you were pregnant I didn't believe you. I thought you were trying to manipulate the situation and have me pity you so I wouldn't finish you off. I'm sorry I took the life of your unborn child, but I swear I didn't kill Supreme. That's my word."

"You a fuckin' lie. Don't try to snake your way out this shit. You the only person that had reason, and is crazy enough to come at Supreme in broad daylight. I know it was you."

"In your heart, if you really believe I was the one, then go 'head and pull that trigger... go 'head," I pressed on.

Precious stepped forward and gripped the gun tighter wanting to blast off so badly, but something held her back.

"You know I'm speaking the truth. Whoever took out Supreme had their own agenda. It was just easy for the blame to fall on me because of what went down between us."

"Well if it wasn't you, then who?"

"Honestly, I don't know, but it wasn't me, that I can promise you."

As Precious digested what I said, neither of us heard the front door opening until she had a gun pointed in her face.

"Bitch, put that gun down before I waste you."

Precious turned to see who had her jammed up, "Yo, I know you ain't part of this bullshit!" she yelled, shaking her head.

"The two of you know each other?" I asked bewildered.

"Yeah, I know Precious very well. I was gonna surprise you, baby, and deliver this bitch to you, but

I see she found her way."

"Ain't this some bullshit! I knew you were a scandalous trick the first time I met you, but I let my guard down and now this." Precious switched her attention back to me. "I can't believe you got this hoe on your team. And Nina, aren't you supposed to be getting married today?"

"What the fuck is going on?" I seethed through clenched teeth.

"Precious, put that fuckin' gun down now and kick it towards me," Nina demanded, ignoring me. Precious did as she said.

"Nina, answer my fuckin' question. How do you and Precious know each other, and what's this about you getting married?"

"Oh, so you don't know about her fiancé? Yeah, I was supposed to be a bridesmaid and everything for this trick. So when did you decide you weren't showing up for the wedding, Nina? Before or after you planned on killing me?" I stared at Nina waiting for her to answer Precious' question. I was hearing all this shit for the first time and it had me completely perplexed.

"If you really want to know how this shit popped off, I'll break it down for you starting from the beginning," Nina began. "I was the one Nico called when he tried and failed to put you six feet under and had to go on the run. I'm sure he never got around to telling you this, but we used to fuck around until he got caught up in yo' silly ass. So when he needed me, I was there so I could prove to him I was a better bitch than you from day one, and he made the mistake choosing you over me. The night you came over to my fiancé's house for dinner, I immediately recognized your face from a picture that Nico still carries around of you. I wanted to kill your ass right there on the spot, but instead I decided that I would befriend you and finish the job that Nico couldn't."

"But Nina, I told you I had put that shit wit' Precious behind me and was moving on."

"Oh, please! And let this bitch get away with ruining your life? She's the reason that we broke up in the first place. She's why you went to jail and you're on the run. You might've decided to let her get away with it, but not me."

"Nah, Nina, you ain't takin' her out. Get that shit out yo' head."

"After everything Precious has done you're still choosing her over me? You're still in love with this poisonous bitch? I'm the one that's been holding it down for you while she's running around like she's queen bee. How can you defend her? I got a good man waiting at the altar for me because I want to be with you."

"Yo, don't put that shit on me. I didn't even know you was engaged. You the one that said you wanted to break out of New York wit' me. I told you to stay here and not put your life on hold to be on the run wit' me."

"You left your fiancé standing at the altar so you could run away with Nico?"

"Precious, shut the fuck up. This ain't none of your business. You're the cause of all this bullshit anyway. Nico and I would be married with children right now if he had never met you."

"Hold up, Nina. Now you're jumping into some other shit. I appreciate all you've done for me, but you can't blame Precious because she had my heart and you didn't. But even if I hadn't met Precious, I still didn't want to wife you. You were always cool people, and that's why when I was jammed up I reached out to you. Sorry shorty, but my feelings never ran deeper than that."

Nina looked crushed by what I said, but it was all true. I had no idea she had created this imaginary love affair between us, but then I didn't know Nina as well as I thought. All this time she had a fiancée that she never mentioned. Honestly, it would've made no difference to me, but the fact she had become cool with Precious and was plotting to kill her behind my back let me know she was unstable and not the woman I thought she was.

"Fuck that! Precious is a dead bitch!" Nina said coldly.

I walked forward. "If you shoot Precious, you have to kill me first," I stated, standing in front of Precious as a shield.

Nina had this bizarre look on her face. She seemed to have mentally checked out. I couldn't believe this was the same woman that I was having a conversation in the kitchen with the other day and planning to let go on the run with me. She was now standing in front of me and her anger for Precious ran so deep that there was a real possibility she would kill me just to get to her. But Nina wouldn't get that chance because a young girl I didn't recognize snuck up behind Nina and shot her from behind. Nina was lying in a puddle of her own blood.

"She's dead," I said after bending down and not feeling a pulse. "Who are you?" I asked the young girl responsible for Nina's death.

"That's Maya. She's a good friend of mine who just saved our lives," Precious said walking over to Maya and taking the gun out of her hand. The girl seemed to be in shock. "Yo, we got to get the fuck outta here. I know somebody heard those gunshots and called the police."

I knew Precious was right so I quickly disappeared into the bedroom, and got my suitcases that were already packed. I wasn't planning on leaving for a couple days to give Nina time to get her shit in order, but that was no longer necessary. I had my money so there was no need for me to wait.

"You couldn't have packed that fast," Precious said when I came out the bedroom.

"I was already packed. I just had to get my luggage from the bedroom closet."

"That's right. Nina did mention the reason she left her fiancée at the altar was so she could run off with you," Precious said sarcastically. "Well, come on, you can ride with us."

"I can't, Precious," I said solemnly.

"What do you mean, you can't?"

"There's too much heat on me right now. You need to go. I'll be in touch."

"You promise?"

"Yes, I promise."

"But where will you go? Do you need money?"

"Precious, I'll be fine. You know how I get down. You just take care of yourself and be careful. Supreme's killer is still out there."

"I'm sorry, Nico. I'm sorry for everything."

I put my finger over Precious lips and kissed her on the forehead before making my exit out the front door.

Chapter 25

Goodbye

I was headed out of town first thing in the morning, but I didn't want to leave without seeing Precious one last time. After all she put me through I was still very much in love with her. I don't think I ever stopped. The rage I was in for what she had done was only camouflaging it. I wasn't sure how Precious felt, but I didn't want to have any regrets so I reached out to her.

"Hello."

"Is anyone around you?"

"Nico, is that you?"

"Judging by the fact that you shouted out my name, I take it that you're alone."

Precious let out a slight chuckle. "Sorry 'bout

that, but I was so surprised to hear your voice. But yeah, I'm alone. How are you?"

"Just keepin' low."

"Are you still in the area?"

"Yeah, I'm tryna tie up some loose ends before I head out of here. If you don't mind, I would like to see you before I leave."

"I wanna see you too. When are you leaving?"

"Tomorrow morning. You think we can meet tonight?"

"Tonight is good."

"Cool. I'll call you around eight to let you know where to come. Make sure you're careful. I can't afford you being tracked by anybody."

"I got you. I'll be waiting for your call."

When I hung up with Precious I knew I had made the right decision. Obviously, we both needed closure and tonight we would get it.

Precious arrived looking beautiful. Her hair was slicked back in a ponytail with a metallic-colored jumpsuit that accentuated every curve. All I wanted to do was take her clothes off, but I tried to maintain my cool.

"Yo, this place didn't even come up in the navigation system," Precious commented of the nondescript spot I was staying at in Staten Island. "The only reason I was able to find it was because I used to hit up this mom and pop soul fool restaurant down the hill every once in awhile. "How did you find this place?"

"I still know a few people who got hideouts."

"This is definitely one of those. Ain't nobody gonna find you here."

"That's the point of a hideout spot. You hope nobody can find it." I smiled.

"True, but it looks nice inside. Hardwood and plush carpet, stainless steel kitchen appliances and a huge open space. You would never know all this was going on from the outside."

"Yeah, it's pretty official for what it is. But I'm ready to break out."

"Have you decided where you're going?"

"Yep, but don't ask me where. If you ever get yourself jammed up and they question you about my whereabouts, I really want you to be able to say you don't know. It's for your own protection."

"Am I gonna ever see you again?"

"I hope. I'll keep in touch from time to time. But if and when I get word that I'm able to show my face again, then you know I'm coming home. New York is truly all I know."

"Nico, you don't have to worry about the charges sticking for shooting me. If they do come at you, I'll tell them I made a mistake and you weren't the person who tried to kill me. I'll get on the stand and testify to that if I have to."

"I don't know what to say. Since I've been on

the run, all I've done was think. Think about my life, the past, and of course, you. It's still hard to believe that this is how everything turned out. When I first got out of jail I was so full of rage and had nothing but contempt towards you. But there is such a thin line between love and hate. And in my heart I never stopped loving you, and even now I wish we could be together and start our life all over again someplace else. But I know that's not possible. I have to clear my name, and maybe then if you still feel the same way, we can try again."

"I can't lie, my feelings for you do still run deep. Just like I hope you've forgiven me for fucking up your life, I've forgiven you for putting a bullet in my chest. I don't know if we can ever be together again, but I do believe the police will find Supreme's killer, whether the person is dead or alive. Then you'll be able to come back and fight the charges they have against you for attempted murder."

"What do you mean, find Supreme's killer either dead or alive? Do you know who took him out?"

"Just like you don't want to tell me where you're going, this is something that I need to keep to myself. But if it all works out, after you disappear, the next time you call me I'll have good news."

"I know how you are, Precious, so I'm not going to pressure you. All I will say is be careful. Whoever took out Supreme is ruthless, and they're playing for keeps. I don't want anything to happen to you,"

I said, now standing within kissing distance of Precious. I lifted her chin and softly brushed her lips against mine. I paused, waiting for Precious' reaction.

"Don't stop," she whispered. Those were the only words I needed Precious to say so I could proceed.

I lifted her up and carried Precious to the bedroom in the back. We both slowly undressed one another and I stood staring at her naked body remembering how good she felt when I was inside of her. I laid her down on the bed and trickled kisses from her soft lips to her neck, breasts, and stomach until reaching the sweetness of her wet pussy. I buried my face in her juices.

Precious let out moans of pleasure that made my dick get even harder. I then stopped and stared at her naked body again, but this time I took my finger and traced the faint scar down the middle of her chest. A pain struck my heart seeing what I had done to the only woman I had ever loved.

Precious pushed my hand away as if she could feel my guilt eating me up inside. She pulled me closer and said, "Baby, put it in. I need that dick inside of me now," she moaned. She sunk her nails deep into my skin as I entered inside of her. Feeling the warmth of her body with each thrust brought back so many memories of how lovely shit used to be between us. She was my woman, my everything back then. Now all I could do was make love to her like it would be our last time. After we both reached the height of pleasure, we climaxed simultaneously and fell asleep in each other's arms.

Early in the morning I could hear Precious get out of bed and get dressed. I pretended to still be asleep because I didn't want us to get caught up in goodbyes. Instead I wanted us to remember how perfect last night was. Before leaving, Precious kissed me on the forehead and softly said, "I love you."

I love you too, I said to myself as I watched Precious walk out hoping it wouldn't be the last time I'd see her again.

Chapter 26

New Beginnings

I woke up at my beachfront condo with the sun beaming down on my face. I had been living in Miami for almost two years and I still wasn't used to waking up to damn near perfect weather everyday. I went outside and stood on the balcony looking at the white sand and crystal blue water. I listened to the waves crash and the birds and seagulls. As beautiful as this shit was, it hadn't taken away my longing to move back home to New York permanently instead of just visiting for business purposes.

During my time in Miami, Precious got her husband back. It came out that Supreme was actually alive. So I was no longer wanted for his murder. Precious also kept her word and changed her story about me shooting her, so the attempted murder charges were dropped too. Precious wanted me to be free to move on with my life because she had moved on with hers. She moved to Beverly Hills with Supreme and they shared a daughter together. We had been in touch a few times and I'd even seen her not too long ago while I was in New York. During that time their baby had been kidnapped. That might've broken any other woman, but not Precious.

Thank goodness they recently got their daughter back and I planned on calling Precious, but I wanted to give her time to be with her family. Supreme was her husband and I respected that no matter how much it hurt. She was no longer mine and I had to accept that fact and move on.

"Nico, come back to bed," I heard Lisa say interrupting my thoughts.

"I'll be there in a minute, baby," I said, turning around before staring back off at the beachfront view. I had met Lisa when I first got to Miami. She was going to school and working part time as a waitress at one of the restaurants on Ocean Drive. Lisa was so young, naïve, and sweet, I almost felt uncomfortable messing with her, but it was those same traits that made me drawn to her. New York women were so sassy and aggressive that dealing with Lisa was easy and relaxing. With the stress I had going on in my life, her personality was perfect and the fact she was easy on the eyes didn't hurt.

"You're back," Lisa said when I got back in the bed. "I wanted to feel you inside of me before I had to leave for work." She smiled, before wrapping her lips around my dick so I could feel the moistness of her mouth. Lisa had my dick rock hard. I brushed my hand against her thighs and her skin was so soft. Instead of waiting for her to finish giving me a blowjob. I flipped Lisa's body over and slid inside. Her pussy was even wetter than her mouth.

"Baby, you feel so good," I moaned, as each stroke got deeper and more forceful.

"Oh Nico, I love you so much," Lisa wailed in pleasure. She wrapped her legs around my back pulling me in closer to feel all my pressure deep inside of her. "Baby, I'm about to cum," she screamed, tugging her legs even tighter around me. Soon after Lisa came, I exploded inside of her. "I wish you could stay inside of me forever," Lisa said caressing the back of my head.

"As good as you feel right now got me feeling the same way."

"I hate to say this, but I have to get up. I don't want to be late for work."

"Why haven't you quit that job yet? I told you weeks ago that you don't need to work there anymore."

"Nico, you already do so much for me. I wouldn't feel right not working. I make really good tips there. No, it's not the kind of money you give me, but it's something."

"I understand. But just know you can always change your mind," I said kissing Lisa on the lips before sliding out of her so she could get out the bed. I watched as she went in the bathroom to take a shower. That was another reason Lisa was special to me, she let me spoil her, but she still wanted her own, no matter how little it was. I was so used to gimmie girls that wouldn't dare show up to a wait-ressing job if they lucked up and found a dude that was paying all their bills but not Lisa, she wasn't like that and I respected her for it.

Since moving to Miami I was able to use the money I made with Nina while I was on the run in New York, to set up shop and get business poppin'. Fernando, whom I had dealings with back when I lived in Brooklyn, set me up with a local Dominican connect and we hit it off lovely. That was another reason why I hadn't moved back to New York. I had an operation going here that almost ran itself. There was so much drug money flowing in Miami that you only had to put in minimal work to reap the benefits.

On my way to meet with my connect I decided to check up on Precious and see how she was doing. "Hi, Precious, I'm happy for you and your family. I wanted to call sooner, but I knew you and Supreme would want some time alone after bringing your daughter home."

"Nico, thank you so much. I'm glad that you called. I was wondering if I would hear from you again. I..."

"Precious, are you there?" I could hear some ruckus like the phone had dropped, but I wasn't sure. I kept screaming out her name, but got nothing. I hung up and called back but after ringing a few times it went to voicemail. "Maybe Supreme walked in or something and she didn't want him to know she was talking to me," I thought out loud as I made a right turn on Biscayne Boulevard headed towards my destination. Although hesitant, I decided it was best for me to wait to hear from Precious instead of calling her back again. If this was about Supreme, I didn't want to cause Precious any problems because she had already been through enough.

"Lisa, I have to go to LA," I said, packing up the last of my things.

"How long will you be gone?"

"I'm not sure. A very good friend of mine is in trouble and I have to go find out what happened to her," I explained, zipping up my bag.

"Let me guess, the she is Precious? Besides Tracy, she's the only female you've ever talked to me about. Since Tracy is dead that only leaves Precious."

"Yes, it is Precious. I called her a few days ago and the conversation ended abruptly. I thought maybe it had to do with her husband Supreme, but a detective has left me a few messages saying he wanted to speak to me about Precious. I've made a few phone calls and I think something bad has happened to her."

"You don't think you should let her husband and the police handle it?"

"They can do whatever they wanna do, but I got access to the streets and might be able to get information they ain't privy to. But I'm not taking no chances, not when it comes to Precious."

"I understand. I know you have a long history with her," Lisa said, putting her head down. I knew Lisa felt some type of way about me breaking out to go chase down my ex, but I always kept it one hundred with Lisa. I didn't sugar coat shit.

"If you want, you can stay here while I'm gone." Although I wasn't in a committed relationship with Lisa, she was the only woman I was dealing with in Miami so I had no issues with her staying here while I was away.

"Okay," she said nodding her head. "I'll stay."

"Cool. I'll leave some money for you, but if anything comes up you know you can call me. I'll also be checking in on you. Be good," I said kissing Lisa on the forehead before heading out to catch my flight.

On my way to the airport I thought about the last time I heard Precious' voice and what she said. I wondered if there was some sort of clue I was missing. All I did know was that Precious would never willingly leave her baby; she had just gotten her daughter back. She had been through hell and came out a survivor. If she was missing, it wasn't voluntarily, she was taken and I would do everything in my power to bring her back home.

Chapter 27

Aaliyah

Three Years Later...

"You're the most beautiful little girl in the entire world," I said holding my daughter Aaliyah. My life had completely changed in the past three years. After going to LA to find Precious, I ended up saving her life after she was beaten and left for dead in a burning house. Once I nursed her back to health, we found ourselves on the East Coast in search of Maya who had kidnapped our daughter. Of course at that time I thought Aaliyah was Supreme's daughter, but that didn't stop me from searching high and low like she was my own child. It's crazy how the universe can play tricks on you because come to find out Aaliyah was mine.

We didn't find out until Aaliyah was involved in a car accident and needed a blood transfusion. That's when Precious told me there was a possibility that I could be her father. She was just a baby and to think there was a chance I could lose her before even knowing if she was my child was the hardest thing I had ever dealt with. It was even harder than losing my father. But Aaliyah survived and through that tragedy I gained a daughter.

"Nico, you're gonna have her so spoiled. You tell her that all the time," Precious shook her head as we sat in the living room at her house.

"That's what a Daddy is supposed to do, ain't that right baby girl," I said, kissing Aaliyah on her cheek.

"Yes, Daddy, that's right." Aaliyah grinned kissing me back.

"It's always hard dropping her off. I wish I could spend every minute of the day with her." I exhaled, watching Aaliyah playing with her doll.

"Mrs. Mills, would you like me to get Aaliyah ready for bed?" the nanny came in and asked.

"Yes, that would be great. It's time for bed Aaliyah," Precious said standing up from the couch and walking over to pick Aaliyah up.

"Let me kiss Daddy goodbye," Aaliyah said, reaching over and giving me a hug and kiss as Precious held her. For a brief moment I wanted to reach over and kiss Precious too. It seemed right, in that moment we felt like a real family. I hated being a part-time Dad and sharing my daughter with another man.

"I guess I should be going," I said to Precious after the nanny took Aaliyah upstairs. "I'll see you next weekend."

"Nico," Precious called out when I was turning to leave. "I never tell you this, but thank you for not ever making this difficult. I know this isn't the ideal situation for you, but you always handle it like a gentleman. I respect you for that."

"You've given me the greatest gift. Instead of stressing about the negatives I try to focus on the blessing that is Aaliyah and you made that possible. Words can't describe how much I love you because of that. I'll talk to you later and give Aaliyah a goodnight kiss for me."

Walking out the door and leaving my daughter seemed to be getting more difficult. Maybe it was because she was getting older, talking more, and our bond was getting stronger. That little girl had become the most important person in my life.

"What are you doing here?" I heard a familiar voice ask as I was getting in my car.

"I was dropping off my daughter," I said to Supreme.

"You love saying that don't you... your daughter."

"That's what Aaliyah is, my daughter. I know it

pains you to say it, but that's the thing about DNA—you can't change it."

"You also can't change the fact that although Aaliyah is your daughter biologically, I'm still her father and Precious is my wife. So I'm good. I doubt we can say the same thing about you."

"Supreme, you might think because you live on this estate, you're a rich superstar and have your family, that you're untouchable. But the thing is you're not the only one. I think I'm untouchable too. See you next weekend." I gave a half smile and drove off.

I was on my way to meet with, Genesis. We were introduced when I was helping Precious to get Aaliyah back. We instantly clicked and became not only business partners but I now considered him a friend. Before meeting up with him, I decided to give Lisa a call since I had been MIA lately. "How you doing pretty girl."

"Better now that I'm hearing your voice," Lisa replied in her usual sweet tone.

"I know I haven't been around the last couple of weeks, but business has been crazy. I was thinking we can go have lunch tomorrow."

"I would like that."

"I'll already be in the city so meet me at the Four Seasons at 2."

"I'll be there. I wanted to talk to you about something anyway."

"Cool, then tomorrow it is. I'll try to call you later on tonight though. If not, I'll definitely see you tomorrow." When I hung up with Lisa I wondered what she wanted to talk to me about. I was thinking that maybe she was becoming restless with our arrangement.

Once I found out Aaliyah was my daughter, I decided to move back to New York when I knew Precious and Supreme would be spending a great deal of time at their estate in New Jersey. When I got settled in I sent for Lisa. At first, she was reluctant about leaving Miami, but once she knew I had an apartment, car, and all her expenses covered she became more comfortable with the idea. Although I made sure she didn't want for anything, the one thing she wanted most I couldn't give her, which was my time. Lisa didn't really have any friends here so if she wanted to go back to Miami, it wouldn't surprise me. I guess I would find out tomorrow, I thought getting out the car to meet with Genesis.

"My man, Nico, you ready to close this real estate deal?" Genesis asked before I even had a chance to sit down and get comfortable.

"When it comes to making money you know I'm always ready for that," I said walking over to the bar and pouring myself a drink.

"I knew you would be. I'm having a dinner to-morrow night. I need you here."

"Tomorrow... that was fast. How did you put it together so quickly?"

"Once I got the green light from you that you wanted in on the deal I pressed go. Money talks so those wall street cats were ready to make it hap-pen."

"I'm impressed, Genesis. I knew we could do great business together, but you're turning out to be an even better partner than I thought."

"This is only the beginning my friend. We're going to be making some major moves. By the time we get done, Amir and Aaliyah will be set for life."

"I like the sound of that. On that note, let me pour myself another drink and one for my partner too." I smiled at Genesis, handing him his drink as we clinked glasses.

Chapter 28

I'll Be Good To You

"Nico, I'm pregnant," Lisa said while we were at the Four Seasons Hotel having lunch. She took a swallow of her water and then sat the glass down.

I picked up my glass of wine and took a sip not saying a word for a few minutes. There was no need for me to ask Lisa if the baby was mine because she was probably the most loyal woman I had ever been with.

"I want to have the baby, Nico," Lisa said as if she took my silence as rejection.

"Of course you do and there is no doubt in my mind you're going to be a wonderful mother."

"Does that mean you want me to have the baby?"

"Yes, that's my child you have growing inside of you. I think it's nice Aaliyah will have a little brother or sister."

"You mean that?" Lisa asked sounding surprised by my response.

"I do. I wasn't expecting to be a father again so soon, but you're a good woman Lisa and I'm going to make sure I'm good to you and our baby."

"Nico, you're already good to me. I haven't wanted for anything since the day I met you."

It was easy to be good to a woman like Lisa. I had been dealing with her for over three years. Although I had never made myself exclusive to her she had always been exclusive to me. Because of my business sometimes I would go weeks without seeing her, but whenever I came back around she was right there waiting for me. I made sure she was rewarded for her loyalty. Lisa wanted for nothing and now that she was carrying my child I would give her even more.

"It's only going to get better," I promised Lisa.

"Are you coming by tonight," Lisa questioned.

"I'ma try to. Genesis is having a dinner party tonight that I have to attend. If it's not over too late then yes I'll definitely come by."

"Can I go to the dinner party with you? I've never met any of your friends."

"Lisa, we've talked about this before. The less people know about you, the safer you are especially now that you're carrying my seed. I want you and

217

my baby to be protected."

"Okay. Hopefully you can come by tonight if not then tomorrow."

"For sure. I think it's time to get you out of your apartment."

"Why? I love that loft."

"It's nice for you, but when the baby comes you're going to need a house with a big backyard and a pool because my son or daughter will know how to swim." I smiled.

"You're going to get me a house?"

"Of course. My child will have everything and so will you. Now let's eat lunch."

"Genesis, that was a nice dinner and very productive. I think we definitely closed the deal."

"I think you're right. We keep closing legitimate deals we can give up our drug empire."

"Neva that, man. I'ma die a hustler. It's all I know. I love that shit and it just isn't because it has made me a very rich man. The grind gives me the ultimate high," I admitted.

"I hear you, Nico and honestly I feel what you're saying. This life is addictive, but having a son now to raise I want to make sure that I'm around to see him grow up."

"Yeah, having a child does make a difference. Sometimes I can't believe that I'm a father. I mean finding out that Aaliyah was mine was the best thing that ever happened to me. She's so beautiful just like her mother."

"I guess it's safe to say that you still have it bad for your child's mother."

"Genesis, I've finally accepted that I'll probably love Precious 'til the day I die, but I gotta let that shit burn. She is happily married to Supreme."

"The heart wants what the heart wants, but I'm glad you let that go. It's for the best."

"I agree," I said thinking about Lisa and the baby we were going to have together.

"I haven't seen you in over a week and you show up ready to take me house hunting," Lisa said, shaking her head.

"I'm sorry about that, but after that dinner Genesis had, I end up having to go out of town the next day. But I'm here to make it up to you," I said giving Lisa a kiss. "You're already starting to get that mommy glow."

"You're so full it." Lisa laughed.

"I'm being serious," I said pulling her closer. "So are you ready to go look at some houses?"

"Why not," she said grabbing her purse. "Let's go!"

"I need to take this call. Meet me in the car," I said handing Lisa my keys.

"Okay," she said cheerfully, giving me a quick kiss before leaving. I waited for a few moments to make sure Lisa had gone before answering the call.

"Precious, I'm surprised to hear from you. Is everything okay with Aaliyah?"

"She's great. I was calling because Supreme and I are going away for a couple days and I wanted to see if you wanted to keep Aaliyah. She could stay with Supreme's parents, but I wanted to give you the option first."

"Precious, I would love that. Thank you."

"You're her father and she adores you. I want you to be in her life as much as possible."

"I want that too. While I have you on the phone there is something I want to tell you."

"What is it?"

"You're actually the first person I'm sharing the news with."

"Do I need to sit down for this," Precious joked.

"I'm having a baby." Precious went dead silent. "Precious, are you there?" I finally asked after not hearing a word from her for a couple of minutes.

"I didn't even realize you had a girlfriend," she finally said.

"She's not my girlfriend."

"So who is she?"

"She's a girl I've been seeing off and on for the last few years."

"I see. Aaliyah is still so young, I hope you won't stop spending time with her once your new baby comes."

"That will never happen."

"Are you sure?" Precious asked. I could hear sadness in her voice, which surprised me because it let me know she still cared.

"You and Aaliyah are the loves of my life. Nothing or nobody will ever change that."

"I don't know what to say, Nico."

"You don't have to say anything. I know there is no chance for us, but that doesn't change the fact that I'll always love you, Precious."

"I love you too, Nico."

"That woman will always have my heart," I said out loud after ending our call. Precious Cummings was truly the love of my life.

Chapter 29

Look What You've Done

What I thought was supposed to be a happy time seemed to have changed in a matter of weeks. One day Lisa and I were looking at new homes for her, but lately the vibe was off and it was unexpected. Lisa and I never had problems before in our relationship because she didn't question me and played her position. Now all of a sudden she had concerns about Precious and I didn't understand why, especially since she was carrying my child.

"I don't know what you want me to say. I do care about you...."

"But you're still in love with Precious," Lisa said, cutting me off. "I can't deal with this anymore. You're still holding a torch for a woman that has moved on with her life."

"Of course I have love for Precious. We have history and we share a daughter together, but I want to try and make things work with you."

"Oh really, is it because you know Precious has no intentions of leaving her husband or is it because of the baby?"

"Why are you doing this?" I shrugged.

"Doing what... having a real conversation with you? I don't want to be your second choice, or for you to settle for me because of a baby. Nobody even knows about me. I'm a secret. You keep our relationship hidden like you're ashamed of me or something."

"I'm not ashamed of you. With the business I'm in and the lifestyle I'm in, I try to keep my personal life private. I don't want to make you a target."

"Whatever. I used to believe your excuses, but my eyes have been opened. I'm a lot wiser now. I've played my position for so long, believing that my loyalty would prove I was worthy of your love, but I'm done."

"Lisa, stop. Why are you crying?" I said, reaching for her hand, but she pulled away. "I was always upfront with you. I never sold you a dream."

"You're right. I sold myself a dream. More like a fairytale. But when I heard you on the phone with Precious that fairytale died and reality kicked in."

"What phone conversation?" I asked, hoping Lisa was bluffing.

"The one where you told Precious, she and Aaliyah were the loves of your life and nothing would change that, not even the baby you were having with me. It was obvious that was the first time you had ever even mentioned my name to her."

"Lisa, it wasn't like that," I said, stroking my hand over my face. "You didn't hear or understand the context of the entire conversation." I shook my head; hating that Lisa ever heard any of that. "That conversation was over a week ago, why are you just now saying something?"

"Because there was nothing to say. I needed to hear you say those words. I knew what I had to do and I did it."

"So what, you're deciding you don't want to deal with me anymore? It's too late for that. We're having a baby together. You gonna have to deal with me whether you want to or not."

"That's not true."

"Listen, Lisa. I'm sorry you heard what I said to Precious. I know that had to hurt, but again I think you read too much into that. I do care about you."

"Just save it, Nico. You care about me like a puppy," Lisa said sarcastically.

"I get it. Your feelings are hurt and you don't want to have an intimate relationship with me any longer, I have to respect that. But that doesn't change the fact you're carrying my child and I will be playing an active role in their life so I don't want us to be on bad terms. I want to be here for you and our baby."

"You don't have to worry about that anymore. You're free to pursue Precious and not feel obligated to me."

"It's not an obligation. We made the baby together and we'll take care of our child together."

"Don't you get it, there is no baby."

"Excuse me? Are you saying you lied about being pregnant?"

"No, I was pregnant, but..."

"But what, you had a miscarriage?"

"No, I had an abortion."

"You killed my child?"

"No, I aborted mine!"

"That was my child too."

"Fuck you! Fuck you, Nico! You want to stand there and act like you gave a damn about our baby and me. You're such a hypocrite and a liar."

"You had no right to make a decision like that without discussing it with me."

"I had every right. I heard you on the phone confessing your love to another woman and the child you all share together. Making it seem like our baby and me was some unwanted burden. Well now you no longer have that burden. Any child I bring into this world deserves better than that."

"You killed my child because of a phone conversation you overheard. You make me sick. I think I actually hate you."

"Now you know how I feel because I hate you, too," Lisa spit back with venom in her voice.

"You need to go before you meet the same demise as the baby you murdered."

"No worries, I have no intentions of staying. As a matter of fact, I came to say goodbye. I have no reason to stay in New York."

"You're leaving town?"

"Yes, for good. Like I said, there is nothing here for me. I don't want to be in the same city as you. It would be a constant reminder of all the time I wasted, waiting for you," Lisa said, as a single tear trickled down her cheek. "Goodbye, Nico."

I watched with contempt and pain as Lisa walked out the door. I couldn't lie to myself. I almost understood why she chose not to keep our baby. I wasn't in love with Lisa and couldn't see me spending the rest of my life with her. The fucked up part was it had nothing to do with her. Lisa was a good girl, but she was right, my heart still belonged to Precious. But I still hated her for aborting our baby. I guess that made me a selfish man. I wanted Lisa to bless me with another child that I could be a father to, but have her accept that she would never have my heart.

At this moment, it was all insignificant. That chapter was now closed. Lisa was out of my life. In the process she took our child with her and for that I would never forgive her.

Epilogue

Angel

Seven Months Later...

"Look at her, mommy, she is so beautiful," Lisa said, holding her newborn baby in the hospital.

"She is beautiful," her mother said, nodding her head. "What are you going to name her?"

"Angel. She's my little Angel." Lisa smiled.

"That's a beautiful name and she is an angel," Lisa's mother said, admiring her granddaughter. "Lisa, are you okay?" she asked, noticing her daughter becoming pale and a pain-stricken expression on her face.

"I'm getting a headache, but I'll be fine," Lisa

said, trying to shake off the discomfort. "Can you hold Angel for a minute. I need to sit up and catch my breath," Lisa said, handing her baby to her mother.

"I would love to." Her mother smiled, gently rocking Angel.

"I feel a little nauseated," Lisa said, feeling hot.

"Do you want me to get the nurse?"

"No, just get me some water," Lisa said. Before Lisa's mother even had a chance to reach for a bottle of water, her daughter began to vomit. In a matter of seconds Lisa's arms and legs began jerking. Her entire body seemed to be having convulsions."

"Lisa... Lisa... what's the matter baby!" Lisa's mother said, her voice shaking, filled with fear. "Somebody get a doctor!" she screamed out, running to the door and holding her grandbaby close to her chest. "My daughter needs a doctor. She's sick! Somebody help her please!" she pleaded, yelling out as she held the door wide open.

"Ma'am, please step outside," a nurse said, rushing into Lisa's room with a couple of other nurses behind her and the doctor close behind.

Lisa's mother paced back and forth in front of her daughter's room for what seemed like an eternity. "It's gonna be okay, Angel. Your mother will be fine," she kept saying over and over again to her grandbaby. "You know they say babies are healing, and you healing your grandmother's soul right now," she said softly in Angel's ear.

"Ma'am."

"Yes... is my daughter okay?" she asked, rushing towards the doctor.

"Ma'am, your daughter was unconscious then her heart stopped."

"What are you saying?" she questioned as her bottom lip began trembling.

"We did everything we could do, but your daughter didn't make it. I'm sorry."

"No! No! She so young. She's just a baby herself. How did this happen?"

"I'm not sure, but we're going to do an autopsy. It will take a couple of weeks for the results to get back. It could be a placental abruption and amniotic fluid embolism, or a brain aneurysm, we don't know. Again, I'm sorry. Do you want us to contact the father of your granddaughter?" the doctor asked.

Lisa's mother gazed down at Angel, whose eyes were closed and she was sleeping peacefully in her arms. "I don't know who Angel's father is. That information died with my daughter."

"I understand. Again, I'm sorry about your daughter. Let us know if there is anything we can do for you," the doctor said before walking off.

"I just want to see my daughter and tell her goodbye," she said walking into Lisa's room. "My sweet baby girl. You look so peaceful." Lisa's mother rubbed her hand across the side of her face. "Don't you worry. I promise I will take care of Angel. I will give her all the love I know you would have. Rest in peace baby girl."

Follow Angel's Story In Female Hustler....

A KING PRODUCTION
All I See Is The Money...
Female Hustler 2
A Novel
JOY DEJA KING